HUNTED IN VENICE

HUNTED IN VENICE

A SENN MYSTERY

ANDY TRAVIS

First paperback edition December 2022
Book designed by Sarah Lahay

Paperback ISBN: 9789083234229
Ebook ISBN: 9789083234236

To my wife, Jells,
for always sighting the silver lining.

CHAPTER 1

WRONG TIME. WRONG PLACE

"Hell is truth seen too late."

—THOMAS HOBBES

Freezing February was not Nicholas Senn's preferred month to be in Venice. But he had no choice. Laura, his best friend, was missing, and he'd come to find her.

Senn felt unwelcome as his motoscafo water taxi dropped him off at his studio apartment in Ca' dei Regio in San Marco, Venice, at 2 AM.

The rain (now hail) lashed his stern, handsome face as he stood under a flickering streetlight, pressed the unresponsive doorbell with his frozen fingers, and waited.

But a growl in the dark instantly made matters urgent.

Out of the darkness, Senn spotted several stray dogs menacingly approaching him a few feet away. Frustrated *and now* anxious, Senn banged hard on the high vaulted, thick door while preparing to defend himself with his broken folding umbrella.

This time to his relief, he heard muffled footsteps descending from inside the crusty, pink Venetian house.

A groggy middle-aged man opened the door a sliver and grumbled, "You were supposed to be here before 10 PM!"

Senn nodded, slid past the scowling man, and let out a deep sigh as he set his heavy bag down. In the large mirror reclining against the hall, Senn's amber eyes caught a glimpse of his shivering, six-foot frame and his wavy, messy, dark hair that now looked like a wet mop covering his boyish, olive-skinned face.

The 32-year-old was too tired to argue or explain his delay to the poor, sleep-drunk man. Senn apologized and handed his Swiss passport to the man, who took ages to fill out the paperwork before giving him the keys to the fourth-floor, walk-up studio apartment.

The man gazed at Senn as he handed him the keys. "You look familiar. Have you been here before?"

Senn nodded and replied, "Yes. Once. I'm Laura's friend."

The man suddenly became grave and suspicious, narrowed his eyes into slits, and said, "Oh! You know she's disappeared, and the police were here asking questions. They think she might be dead."

Senn clenched his jaw and nodded. "That's why I am here. To find her."

The man's eyes widened with curiosity. "Are you her boyfriend?".

Senn shook his head and said, "No. Just a good friend."

The man's patent frown returned as he bent his head and muttered, "OK, your room's on the top floor," and waved Senn away as he continued filling the forms.

Senn panted up the rickety, carpeted stairs that smelled of stale nicotine as he passed the closed doors of the apartment block, one of which used to be Laura's studio apartment.

She'd disappeared suddenly after failing to show up to work at the Teatro Rossi, a 19th-century opera house in the theatre district where she was busy restoring the rare art and murals in the Teatro.

Senn only found out when he got a call from the Venetian police three days ago asking if he knew where she was. Senn was alarmed to hear they suspected she could be dead without explaining further!

Senn pleaded with the officer on the phone, offered to help, and told them he was an investigative journalist. The wary officer snubbed him, told him to write to the chief of police for permission, and hung up. Senn, quite used to such deflective tactics, decided to fly to Venice and hoped to convince the chief in person and join the search for Laura.

Senn was not *entirely* surprised by the call.

He'd had a premonition about Laura the night before the police called him. Senn recalled the moment it happened as he turned the key in his attic flat.

After living in London for a decade with his Italian (now) ex-girlfriend, he'd sold the flat there and just moved into a loft apartment in Prinsengracht, Amsterdam. He was unpacking his books and papers when a polaroid slipped and fell to the ground. It was a photograph of him and Laura getting wasted in London a few summers ago at their jointly hosted farewell party.

Back then, Laura was an art history reporter at the London office of the *International Tribune*, a prestigious newspaper where Senn was also an investigative journalist. They had worked there for over three years and had become close friends. They resigned on the same day for different reasons and had decided to host a joint farewell.

Senn picked up the polaroid and smiled at it fondly when he felt his eyes dilate, and a strong shock wave riddled his body.

He was having a *soul flash*—Senn's secret unwitting *(albeit erratic and painful)* superpower.

He saw a woman who resembled Laura wearing a black, hooded jacket standing on a stage in the rain.

She looked distraught. It was dark, and the place felt remote. Then the image disappeared, leaving Senn cold and shivering. He felt weak with a throbbing ache in his stomach. The feeling lasted a few minutes and then faded.

He'd tried calling Laura immediately, but her phone went to voicemail. Then the Venetian police called him the following day.

Soul flashes had become part of his life since they started after a bizarre accident that nearly killed him.

For his eighteenth birthday, his buddies (all a few years older and tougher), after their workout in the gym, gifted him a 5 mg dose of Psilocybin mushrooms as an initiation into psychedelics.

Senn, desperate to impress the friends of his machismo, pretended the dose did not affect him and, to prove it, walked out into the stormy night to the Olympic pool in the complex, climbing to the top of the 10-meter-high diving board to show them his steady nerve.

While his friends watched, splitting their sides with laughter, Senn undressed down to his boxers in the lashing rain, balanced on the edge of the board, and prepared to dive.

At that instant, a lightning bolt lit up the sky and stuck Senn with a deafening crack. Senn lost consciousness, and his limp body fell 10 meters, slamming hard into the water.

The shock was so severe that Senn lay in a coma for three days, with a fifty-fifty chance of survival.

But he survived. And within days, he noticed this uncanny psychic power, which gradually unfolded in him as he grew up.

The best way he could describe visions in a soul flash was haphazard sensory jolts of cryptic premonitions pointing at mysterious future occurrences that he could ignore or (invariably) investigate. It was painful to experience a soul flash as they always occurred without warning, leaving him drained and exhausted.

He kept tight-lipped about his power to avoid becoming an oddity among his peers and friends (including Laura). He was determined to live an ordinary life despite this occult appendage.

Senn unpacked his bags, stripped out of his freezing wet clothes, and got under the hot shower to try and feel his toes again. He was glad he'd found a room in the same building as Laura to feel her aura and try to find clues in her room by asking the neighbors. The last time he had been here was in the summer, a year back, and he had great memories of hanging out and exploring Venice with her and her friend Sophie.

It had already been four days since her disappearance, and he was annoyed that the police had not been able to find anything so far. Or maybe they had; he needed to speak to them after he convinced the police chief to let him join the search.

But his first meeting tomorrow was at the theatre where she worked and to talk to the creative director, Stephan Conti, who had reported her missing to the police and had already requested to meet Senn.

He'd sent him a puzzling cryptic email.

His mail was short and read, *"Dear Mr. Senn, I urgently need your help. Laura, your friend, has gone missing, and I need to tell you something about it in private. Please come to Venice immediately, as I am worried for her safety. I prefer you not call me but come to the Teatro Rossi first before meeting the police."*

Senn did not trust this guy one bit. Laura had briefly messaged him about her eccentric boss, how he made his troupe work to the bone and his exacting attention to detail and mastery. Senn remembered her being impressed and wary of his genius in the same breath.

But Senn was suspicious about Stephan's mind games.

He seemed overzealous in clarifying his point of view. The Venetian police had already met him once, and his alibi checked out because his mother vouched for him being home with her on the night Laura went missing.

Why did Stephan think it was safe to share evidence with him, not the police? Senn wondered as he switched off the bedside light to catch a few hours of restless sleep.

CHAPTER 2

THE SUSPICIONS OF THE SUSPICIOUS DIRECTOR

"A thing is not necessarily true because a man dies for it."

—OSCAR WILDE

Senn woke up to squawking seagulls on the red terracotta rooftops outside his fourth-floor canal view window in Venice. It was 6 AM, and he was in no mood to get out from under his warm duvet. His body ached and felt feverish. Maybe he had the flu despite his double vaccine! After all the global lockdowns and personal meltdowns of 2020, Senn was determined to make 2021 fare better.

Senn checked his phone for any messages from Laura. He had been watching all her social media ever since she vanished. But there was no activity on the platforms except for worried messages from friends and family wondering about her whereabouts and wishing her well.

The last post from Laura was five days ago, around midnight, after rehearsals at the Teatro Rossi. Stephan was feverishly directing his troupe to perform Aladdin in a couple of months when the season began at the end of March.

Stephan had made everyone work late continuously for many nights in a row, and she looked tired but smiled and posted a selfie that read, "12 hours a day! 5 days in a row! Stephan is Satan! #Exhausted!"

But suddenly, after that night, everything stopped. Her phone was switched off a few minutes after that post and never restarted.

Sleep-deprived and restless, Senn scanned his YouTube channel for traffic. He had recently launched his Youtube channel, Probe. He had a growing following of over 10,000 fans, and some of his stories were gaining traction, crossing a million views for the first time.

Senn had gotten tired of the budget cuts and arm-twisting he faced from his bosses to water down his reporting on many occasions due to pressure from the advertisers. So a year ago, in the middle of the pandemic, Senn finally ended his procrastination, quit his day job, and launched Probe.

It was a subscription and donation-based platform where he reported on issues he thought were underreported and needed society's greater attention and action.

His latest story featured teenage refugees escaping Turkey, Iran, and Afghanistan and coerced into modern-day slavery. In the vlog, he exposed a ring of gangs linked directly to wealthy upper classes worldwide who openly exploited these youths into sex slavery and organ removal to service the rich.

It was not the sexiest topic for the algorithms to curate. Still, at 32, Senn was finally living up to his promise to be an independent journalist unencumbered by political pressure or working a 9–5 job.

Money was a trickle, but Senn had saved enough cash to last him a couple of years without a regular income. He hoped it would be enough time for his online brand to replace his monthly expenses. He was working flat out to create content for his channel, but he put all that on hold when he heard about Laura.

Senn showered and pulled on his fraying grey Harvard Business School alum jersey. After graduating in 2012, instead of a cushy corporate career, Senn opted for a grittier life as a news reporter to satisfy his passion for storytelling and fighting social injustice.

Senn took his coffee and climbed the narrow wooden steps through the skylight out to the terrace. The breezy sniper perch was ideal for watching Venice's Grand

Canal come alive at Ponte dell'Accademia and calming his nerves before meeting Stephan.

Senn was curious for obvious reasons but also keen to know Stephan more. Senn had heard rather strange things about him from Laura, who once described Stephan as a *crazy enigma.* When Senn had tried to probe further, Laura had shied away from the topic.

Senn reached the Cafe Alberotti on the other side of the Grand Canal five minutes late. Stephan was waiting for him inside at a corner table, looking out at the passing Vaporetto as his eyes nervously darted at each person who passed by the half-open café door.

Even though this was their first encounter, Senn instantly recognized his famous face.

His clean-shaven, oval, bald head; pale, taut skin stretched tightly over his sharp protruding jawline; and piercing black eyes dissected the world from behind his thin, round, gold-rimmed glasses. He sat there looking calm on the surface while his raised heels rocked his lean legs with impatience under the table. He was the perfect caricature of the dark, mysterious Venetian theatre world.

Everyone in the Venetian art world knew Stephan Conti—aka *the Sadist of the Venetian stage.*

Stephan Rossi was the insomniac and perfectionist director of the Teatro Rossi, one of the iconic theatres in the Venice theatre district. He was infamous for his meticulous attention to detail in his stage performances, where he insisted on rehearsing every act to exhaustion for himself and his actors. His actors laughed and called his rehearsals `going to the Gulag'—referring to the forced labor camps established during Joseph Stalin's soviet reign.

Yet, he was worshipped like a god by his actors.

"Hi, Stephan, I'm Senn," Senn said as he warmly extended his hands toward Stephan.

Stephan's eyes froze and bore into Senn's face as if dissecting him down to the atom. He stood and towered over Senn as he shook his hand. Senn was six feet tall, but Stephan was at least three inches taller than him.

Stephan frowned as they sat across the table and asked, "Are you here with someone else?"

"No, it's just me. Why?" Senn mumbled, taken aback.

"Because you're wearing a rose perfume that I normally don't expect on men," replied Stephan in a dull, matter-of-fact tone, his eyes riveted on Senn.

Senn looked confused and was about to object to his suspicion when he remembered he'd helped the florist on the other end of the bridge put a box of freshly cut roses on the ground that was about to topple off the delivery van.

Senn, impressed with Stephan's acute sense of smell, explained why he might be smelling of roses, to which

Stephan nodded without breaking a crease on his blank face, "Surprising. Yet possible."

Then without flinching, he changed the subject, and his eyes regained their nervous dart as he said, "I'm sure Laura's happy you're here to find her, but there's something I have to tell you that you can't tell anyone."

Senn found Stephan's eccentric behavior disturbing yet riveting as he nodded and leaned forward, curious.

Stephan lifted his long, bony index finger to his lips and whispered, "Laura was being followed...by a ghost."

CHAPTER 3

"SHE SAID SHE'D BEEN MURDERED."

"Men occasionally stumble over the truth, but most of them pick themselves up and hurry off as if nothing had happened."

—WINSTON S. CHURCHILL

"What do you mean?" Senn asked, looking bewildered at Stephan.

Stephan kept silent as his hooded eyes bore into Senn like glowing embers on a cold winter's night. His shining, stretched scalp quivered with dancing twitches around his eyes as he tried to cover a slight tremor in his right hand with his left. He looked much older than his forty years by at least a decade.

"She told me she could communicate with dead people," replied Stephan with a slight tremble in his voice.

Senn's head tilted, and his eyes narrowed as he tried to hide his amusement at hearing this.

Senn knew Laura was a *wannabe* clairvoyant. She'd read a lot on the occult and tried to show off her channeling and palmistry powers on him sometimes between the second and fourth glass of wine every time they met. But not a single prediction was correct!

But Senn used to fake a few. 'Wow! How did you know that?' to bolster her enthusiasm.

"Really?" asked Senn, pretending to look shocked at the revelation and empathize with the ghostly grimness on Stephan's face. "What did she see?" he prodded Stephan.

Stephan looked blankly at the selfie-obsessed gondolas in the Grand Canal, crossed his arms, and whispered in a chant-like hum, "She said she encountered a ghost in the Teatro. The ghost was a woman who told Laura that someone murdered her in the basement."

Senn felt something flicker in the light in the water. Before he could look, the transparent object dived and dissolved into the canal.

Senn fell silent.

Maybe Laura's training and desire were bearing fruit. Perhaps she *was* finally becoming a channel for unquenched souls.

Stephan continued in a nervous gust of words, "The girl, or whatever it was that spoke to Laura, told her that she's been waiting to speak to someone and tell them what happened to her. The ghost told her to return to the Teatro and bring a flashlight next time." Stephan paused, stared intently at Senn, and spoke sternly, " Mr. Senn, I don't believe in ghosts, but I was worried about Laura. She sounded pretty scared when she called me."

"Did Laura say anything else?" Senn pressed Stephan to glean more info.

"Not much more," Stephan replied. "She wanted to meet me to discuss it further. But that was the day before she disappeared." Stephan looked exhausted as he leaned back and arched his neck to release the pressure in his stiff spine.

"But why have you not reported this to the police?" Senn pressed him in an urgent tone.

Stephan clenched his jaws and replied, "I detest the police, Mr. Senn. The police would think I'm mad if I repeated what Laura told me. It made no sense to me either but more importantly, then I'll be a suspect." Stephan raised his voice, exasperated, and said, "I have no time for this right now. After two years of excruciating wait, I am about to premier Aladdin in the Rossi, and I can't get bogged down by the police."

But then Stephan suddenly lowered his voice, stared directly at Senn, and whispered, "But I want you to find out about this woman or ghost Laura heard. It could help you find Laura."

Before Senn could react and ask him why he'd had to wait two years, he spotted from the corner of his eye a small-framed, middle-aged lady with cotton-candy-soft white hair and large, gold, metal-framed glasses entered the cafe and strode straight towards them. Senn sensed her presence as she gave him a genial dimpled smile and then looked at Stephan and, putting her hand on his shoulder, said in a gentle voice, "Sorry to disturb you, son, but don't we have to go shopping for the party tonight?"

Stephan had missed the lady entering the cafe. He jumped at her voice and looked a little sheepish as he turned and looked at her and replied, "Yes, Mama, I'm ready."

He looked at Senn and said, "Mr. Senn, this is Mia, my mother. Mama, this is Mr. Senn, Laura's friend and a journalist who's come here to look for her."

Mia turned to look at Senn, her kind, pretty, slightly wrinkled face instantly filled with concern and sympathy.

Mia's tone changed, and in a slightly quivering, high-pitched voice, she said, "How interesting! How interesting! Mr. Senn, it's a pleasure to meet you. Stephan has been worried to death about Laura." Mia tenderly glanced at a flustered Stephan and then locked her gaze on Senn again.

"It's very worrying. Very worrying. Did you know Laura well?" Mia asked in a semi-inquisitive and semi-compassionate manner.

"Laura is my closest friend, madam," Senn replied. "We worked together in London before she moved here."

Mia extended her hand to Senn and said, "I am so sorry, Mr. Senn, to hear that. You must be so worried. We are all very worried about Laura. Have you spoken to the police yet?"

Senn reached out and shook Mia's hand but instantly realized that her palm was cold and hard as a rock. It was a prosthetic arm but looked realistic and well-matched in her skin tone and body shape.

Mia, who seemed quite used to the kind of reaction she saw on Senn's face, smiled and remarked, "Yes, it's a prosthetic arm. I lost the original in a boating accident many years ago."

Senn grimaced, feeling her pain, shook her hand gently, and replied, "So sorry to hear that."

Mia smiled and raised her left hand. "God knew I was left-handed, so he thought I could donate the other to someone who needed it more than me."

Senn laughed politely at her self-deprecating sense of humor and looked across at Stephan, who was also beaming, looking proud to have such a brave mama.

"So, have you spoken to the police yet?" Mia repeated her question.

"Not yet," replied Senn. "I have an appointment with the chief of police next. I need to get his permission to investigate the case. But I came to meet Stephan first."

Mia nodded in sympathy and then closed her eyes, bent her head, said a silent prayer for a few seconds, and kissed the silver cross around her neck. Opening her eyes and, gently patted Senn's outstretched arm. "God will clear the way."

CHAPTER 4

"THIS IS A POLICE STATION, NOT A CAFE."

Senn could tell Mia was worried about Laura.

After a polite glance at Senn, Mia turned and walked towards Stephan, already standing alert at the ornate cafe door.

Senn still had many unanswered questions for Stephan, but Mia looked determined to take her son shopping.

Senn watched as the mother and son disappeared into their classy indigo-striped lacquered motorboat and merged with the melee of boats scurrying around in the freezing February waters of the Grand Canal.

Senn had not had time to soak in the place when he arrived. The morning sun was flooding through the bay windows of the cafe and lighting up the gaggle of photographs on the wall of celebrities that had been there before and sat under the enormous grand chandelier that hung from the high vaulted ceiling.

The weathered bartender, who resembled one of the faded oil paintings on the wall, stared at Senn holding a broom, eager to start cleaning the place. They had officially not opened for business yet. It looked like they were doing Stephan a favor. Being famous had its perks, Senn mused as he glanced at the gilded wall clock as it clicked into a synchronistic 10:10 AM.

It was time to meet the Venetian Carabinieri boss, commanding officer Colonnello Francesco Taino.

Senn was nervous about this meeting. He had read up on Col. Taino and knew he was a decorated officer with the Medal of Valor, the highest in Italy, for prosecuting some famous Sicilian mafia bosses.

He also had a fierce reputation for being proud and protective of his officers and their working methods. Senn knew he had to be very persuasive to stand any chance of being allowed access to the search for Laura.

Senn walked into the imposing red brick building at the corner of Campo Zaccaria. A handsome young officer who spoke English with an eastern European accent introduced himself as Captain Mattey and asked him to be seated as the colonel was returning from a meeting.

Senn felt like a lost tourist as he waited.

Sitting next to him was a little girl, no more than seven or eight years old, who sat dangling her legs from the chair, looking sad and forlorn. Sitting next to her was a rather stern-looking middle-aged lady who kept looking impatiently at her watch.

On inquiring, the woman said the little girl had separated from her parents in St. Marco Square, and police brought her here, but the parents had been found and were on their way to collect her.

On the spur of the moment, Senn decided to entertain her while they waited. He put his hand in his pocket, pulled out a 50-cent coin, put it on his palm, and slowly moved it towards the girl so she could see it. She kept her head down, but now her eyes were on Senn's palm and the coin.

Senn smiled and waved his other palm over the coin and made a whooshing sound, and the coin vanished. The girl's eyes lit up, and for the first time, she looked up at Senn; a sliver of a smile spread across her angelic face.

Senn kept his eyes fixed on her, made another whooshing sound, and waved his hands madly, but this time added a mad muttering chant as he jiggled his body from head to toe. He knew he looked ridiculous because it made the girl giggle.

Senn abruptly stopped and showed her his empty palms again, which he closed and rubbed hard before moving them in front of the girl's face, who was mesmerized by Senn's antics. He slowly opened his palm, and the coin was magically back.

The lady escorting the girl gasped in unison with the little girl, who gave Senn a big, shy smile and giggled with delight.

Just then, a panicked young couple entered the station, rushed towards them, and hugged their daughter in utter relief and joy.

In all this commotion of a teary reunion, Senn had missed the entrance of Colonnello Francesco Taino. Senn caught a glimpse of him staring at him sternly as he passed.

A few minutes later, Senn was summoned.

Senn walked into a plush, marble-columned, spacious room with luxurious velvet sash windows with views out to the bustling canal. In the far corner of the room sat the Colonnello, busy signing some documents while a nervous junior officer waited, arms tightly crossed behind his back.

Taino spoke in a whisper that sounded more like a sneer to the officer and then dismissed him as he shifted his gaze to Senn.

"Mr. Nicholas Senn," the Colonnello said in a voice that had a rasp from many decades of Cigar smoking.

Before Senn could answer, the colonel continued in the same monotone, "I saw you hugging and kissing people in the lobby as I was coming in. I hope you remember that you are in my police station and not some cheap cafe."

CHAPTER 5

GOOD THINGS COME WITH CONDITIONS

"What is a friend?
A single soul dwelling in two bodies."

–ARISTOTLE

Senn was not expecting much but wasn't expecting this passive-aggressive reception from the head of the Venetian police.

Francesco Taino's angry blue eyes stared viciously at Senn as he waited for him to respond. The man was in his mid-fifties and looked like a former bodybuilder with a clean-shaven head and a stylish grey beard to complete the daunting profile.

Senn thought for a second and then replied in a slightly defensive tone, "Sir, with all due respect, I am well aware that this is your office and not a cafe, but I was just keeping a little girl entertained while she waited for her parents."

Francesco looked down at his desk and shook his head in exasperation. Senn instantly regretted his words. He kicked himself and thought, *Getting defensive in the first sentence—stupid start, dude!*

Senn was about to apologize and explain what he meant when Francesco rose from his chair and walk towards Senn while observing him with deep suspicion. Senn felt slightly uncomfortable but tried to look calm while Taino sized him up like a school principal on his morning assembly rounds, looking for dirt in the nails or the missing elastic in one sock. He sat across from him on the sofa where Senn was seated, looked down at Senn's shoes, then at his faded, old faithful North Face backpack, and then back at his confused face and muttered something in Italian.

Then in a sudden move, Francesco stretched out his giant padded palm at Senn, and his barbed face cracked open into a beaming, boyish grin. "Francesco Taino, delighted to meet you, Senn."

Senn, surprised by this volte-face move, tentatively looked at Francesco, unsure of his mood. Seeing Senn's confused face, Francesco burst out laughing like a kid who's managed to scare his friend in a dim-lit hallway.

His deep, husky laugh resounded around the high ceilings of his office, making them feel taller than they already were and making Francesco look a little less menacing in his bulging, star-encrusted, crisp, black uniform.

"I was just breaking the ice, soldier." Francesco laughed as he shook Senn's hands vigorously and kept squeezing them until they ached a little before letting go. "I saw you entertaining the little girl. Nice one. Nice one! My team had warned me you were coming to ask for the impossible, but they didn't tell me about your deadly magic tricks!"

This time he looked at Senn graciously. "Well done," he continued. "We love good Samaritans like you. I tell the public that we, the police, would be powerless without their vigilance and compassion for the community. The more they look out for each other, the easier it is for us to do our job."

With his knuckle-crushing handshake and childish sense of humor, Senn felt unprepared for what to expect next from the eccentric colonel yet felt at ease in his company.

Taino leaned back in his chair and, with a furrowed brow, said, "So what can I do for you, Mr. Senn?"

Senn nodded and steadied himself to *ask for the impossible.*

Clearing his throat, Senn said, "Sir, my name is Nicholas Senn. I am here to ask for permission to assist you in the search for my best friend, Laura." Senn continued without letting the Col. interject, "I am an investigative journalist. I used to work for the *International Herald* in London for seven years and now have my own digital media company. I have a lot of experience in international crime and have worked in many countries with agencies, including the FBI, Mossad, and Interpol. I want to assure you that this investigation for me is strictly personal, and I have no profit motives whatsoever."

Taino listened calmly and, before Senn could start talking again, raised his hands and motioned Senn to be quiet.

Staring straight into the pleading eyes of Senn, he said, "I can't let you into Venetian police business, Mr. Senn. It's not allowed."

Senn's heart sank. This was going to be a short meeting.

Then with a pause, the colonel continued. "*However*," he paused and stood to walk to a cabinet and pull out a file, "I've watched and read some of the work you've done. Some of the criminal cases you've investigated and solved are ingenious and impressive."

Senn was surprised that the busy chief knew of his work.

Taino continued.

"And I know this is personal for you. So, I will make you an offer you can't refuse." Taino winked. "I will let you be an *international observer* in the investigation. You can't ask for classified information *unless we offer it.* But you *are* welcome to search for your friend; we will not object."

Senn let out a sigh of relief.

Taino continued, "I'll try to help you as much as I can legally. I can't share confidential info, but I can give you an overview of what we are doing and who is helping us. OK?"

Senn nodded. "I understand, colonel. I am here to help as well, and as you said, this search is not just urgent but personal to me."

Francesco smiled. "Allora, We've conducted a countrywide search for Laura since last week but haven't gotten anything back from the network yet. Interpol is also in the loop. Since Laura was English, we're also taking the help of British intelligence on the case. We have a detailed record of all her social media activity until the evening she went missing. But we haven't found anything that suggests she was planning vacations or traveling for work."

Taino paused, looked at Senn, and, in a grave tone, said, "All I know so far is that she was busy preparing for their upcoming musical with Stephan Conti. We've grilled him, but his alibi checked out as he was home with his mother, Mia, on the night Laura went missing."

"Yes," Senn said. "I met Stephan this morning before seeing you."

Francesco nodded. "Yes, I know. He's been quite open with us so far. In fact, he gave us your name and asked us to contact you." Francesco lowered his voice. "But I know he's not telling us everything. He's famous in Venice but keeps his private life very secretive. Did he tell you something helpful?"

Senn hesitated. Protecting his sources as an investigative journalist was his right and responsibility, even though he was there to find his friend this time. "Nothing that would give me a clear idea of where Laura might be. No, sir."

Francesco nodded and looked at his watch when there was a knock on his door; his secretary informed him that his next appointment was waiting for him.

Francesco thanked the officer, turned to Senn, and said, "I have to stop our meeting here, unfortunately, but I don't have any more for you right now. I have asked one of my agents to contact you to help you while you are in Venice. She will find you. I can't say any more at this time."

Senn stood, slung his backpack over his shoulder, shook Taino's hand (this time a bit more prepared for the knuckle crush), and said his goodbyes. Even though they had not found anything substantial, he felt hopeful that he would be well supported in his investigations.

As he reached to open the door, the colonel walked up behind him, put his hands on Senn's shoulders, and whispered, "One important thing, the agent is my niece. She told me not to tell you that, but *she's my angel*, So take good care of her."

CHAPTER 6

TANGLED IN A VENETIAN MAZE

Senn walked out of the police station, downcast and frustrated with the lack of substantial leads on Laura.

The police chief was friendly but did not seem too concerned about the lack of new information from any sources.

The lack of urgency bothered Senn a lot.

It had already been five days since Laura went missing. Taino had promised him an agent (his niece!), but when and where he would meet her was ambiguous.

It was almost noon, and the winter sun played hide-and-seek with thunderclouds gathering over the city. The cold wind had picked up a notch as well. Senn zipped up his jacket and pulled the hood over his head as he walked towards the Vaporetto.

He wanted to go to the Teatro Rossi and map the place out. The only clue he had to go with at this point was the story of the *ghost of the Teatro,* who seemingly told Laura to come back to the place with a flashlight to see her murder re-enacted. Senn had a flashlight in his backpack, so he was ready if she reappeared.

Senn reached the San Marco-San Zaccaria ferry terminal and checked the timing for the next ferry to Accademia. Three minutes. Teatro Rossi was within walking distance from the ferry stop.

It was starting to rain a little by now. Senn was the first to board the water bus, which was unusually heaving with tourists and locals for the time of day. He squeezed past some of them and found an empty corner with an uncramped wide-angle view of Venice, the winged lion.

Senn paused his spooling mind to admire the city he loved.

Venice, to him, was like a medieval mirage still afloat in the modern age. He loved her architectural grandeur, the magnificent criss-cross of grand canals, and the densely knit alleyways hiding the city's secrets under her embroidered cloak. He loved her resilience to the rising tides, the flood of eat-and-run tourists, and even the annoyance of giant, smoky cruise liners passing through during the summer. Venice seemed to bear it all with a benefic smile.

From the vantage point of his Vaporetto, Senn saw a gaggle of young guys and girls heading to a costume party. Senn half expected to spot the ecstatic face of Laura to pop up and scream at him for being late for the party.

It was always a riot when he hung out with Laura. She could sniff out a party in the middle of a desert. There was always a bash to go to or to help host. Laura was a part-time DJ; she knew all the cool clubs and DJs in whichever town she visited.

Senn met Laura five years ago at her 24th birthday bash in Soho, London. Back then, he'd just joined the *Tribune*, and Laura freelanced with them. They'd hit it off after they discovered a shared passion—Tango. Senn and Laura set the dance floor alight but also set the foundation for a deep friendship to blossom between the two. Senn was still hanging onto a woman who eventually broke his heart, and Laura was dating her flying instructor. Even after they became single again, their friendship remained platonic, and he cherished that simplicity amid his otherwise chaotic life.

Senn's daydream ended when a young priest bumped into him and tried to jostle his way past the crowded boat toward the exit. He was being rather un-priestly in pushing the passengers as he moved. He had a winged tattoo on the back of his palm, which felt odd to Senn, given his attire. Senn missed the man's face but saw his hair tied back in a ponytail as he disembarked in a hurry.

Senn forgot about the ungainly priest as he stepped off and focused on orienting himself towards the Teatro. From the Accademia ferry stop, it was a five-minute walk, so Senn plugged his headphones in, set his playlist to

Billie Eilish languidly singing "Lost Cause," and headed for Stephan's Teatro Rossi.

Senn turned the corner into a narrow-arched passageway under the houses that stretched fifteen meters until it joined the main Rio Terrà Foscarini. Senn had barely gone a few meters when a shadow darted towards him, and before he could react, he felt a vicious blow to his head. The force of the impact made Senn's knees buckle, and he fell flat on the cobbled stone pavement with his backpack open, and its contents strewn all around.

Senn had been mugged in broad daylight before, which is what he imagined this to be. Senn tried to get a good look at the man despite of his dizzy vision and was alarmed to see it was the same priest he'd bumped into on the boat!

This time, the only difference was the added wooden club, knife in his hands, and a mask across his face. The blow's intensity had rendered Senn lifeless and entirely at the man's mercy. The man lowered his knife under Senn's chin and raised it until they were face to face. Senn looked into a masked face with cold, light grey eyes seething down at him in anger.

But then the man did something that shocked Senn. In a heavy Italian accent that echoed in the dark alley, he said, "Senn, "Stay away from the Teatro."

The man smiled at Senn's shocked face, winked, and vanished around the corner.

Senn lay there for a few seconds, making sense of what had happened. The back of his head throbbed, and warm blood oozed as he touched his scalp.

But just then, he heard someone running towards him from the other end of the tunnel. This time, Senn reached for his hidden ankle knife and braced himself for another attack.

"Mr. Senn, are you alright?" This time, it was a woman's voice that sounded full of concern. Senn heard his name again, ricocheting off the graffitied, grimy walls and then saw the outline of a young woman in white sneakers and a padded winter jacket tentatively approaching him.

"Mr. Senn, are you alright?" she repeated worriedly.

"Who are you?" Senn asked, confused but still poised to strike in defense.

"I'm Anna. Anna Accardi. Colonel Taino's niece."

CHAPTER 7

ANNA, THE SECRET STUDENT

The blood was still oozing from the back of Senn's head as Anna helped him collect some of his stuff from the ground where the mugger had attacked him.

Senn made a mental note of the street name, *Calle Pompea*. It was a quirky habit of Senn's to remember the name of the place where someone or something ever attacked him.

The habit was born a decade ago when he was snapping a picture of the colorful street signage of the famous Istikal street in Istanbul when he felt a gun on the back of his head, and the man stole his SLR camera and backpack. Since then, street signs and Senn have retained an uncanny attachment.

Senn smiled at Anna, extended his grubby hand, and said, "Nice to meet you, Anna. How long have you been following me?"

"Since you left the police station," she replied with a broad smile, shaking his hand firmly without apologizing for tailing him, which confirmed Senn's hunch that he had eyes on him since he got out of Col. Taino's office.

In her carefree shoulder-length hair, black leather jacket, and jeans, this innocent looking five-feet, few-inches-tall, Anna Accardi looked more like a nerdy girl out of a college library than a Venetian police officer.

Ignoring his suspicions, Senn shook her hand and replied, "Nice to meet you, officer."

Anna looked surprised and shot back, "No, I'm not a police officer, Mr. Senn. I'm a student studying Criminal Psychology at the university here in Venice. My uncle suggested I follow this case for my master's thesis." Then she paused and sheepishly added, "And help you find your friend."

Senn tried to hide his grimace of disappointment.

Taino had peddled him a budding professor!

He was in the middle of a frantic search for Laura and getting attacked and threatened in broad daylight at knifepoint. And all the police chief could muster was his niece, armed with a pen and notebook, on a deadline to complete her master's thesis!

But it was not Anna's fault. It was Taino's call, and Senn intended to call him and ask for someone more professional to aid him after he got rid of Anna. He steadied his gaze away from Anna's face to hide his frustration and said, " Are you sure you want to work with me?"

The pain from the head blow was throbbing like a strobe light.

Senn tried to remain polite and said, "Look, Anna, I don't want to sound rude, but I don't know if you working with me is such a good idea. A guy just attacked and threatened me. I have no idea where my friend is, and this case is not as straightforward as you might think." Senn took a deep breath and ended, "I suggest you're better off finding a different project. If you speak to your uncle, I'm sure he'll get you something better than this case."

Anna listened with a big frown but did not look deflated at Senn's words. She took on an even more determined look.

Squinting her grey eyes under her broad forehead, she raised her voice and said, "But, Mr. Senn, I know a lot about this case. I've been studying it intently for the last week, so I can help you with details you might not know about the investigation. I also worked in the Missing Foreigners department for a month last year as an intern, so I still know someone in the department and can get access to all their files if we want. And most importantly, my uncle has said I can talk to him whenever I want if we need his help." Anna spoke fast and earnestly in perfect English with just a hint of an Italian accent to suggest her Venetian roots.

She stood firm, facing Senn in the middle of the busy street, cheeks flushed in defiance, her arms akimbo, trying to convince him of her true value despite her missing officer badge.

Senn was unsure about the collaboration and even started to suspect that this could be the colonel's way of keeping an eye on him.

But Senn did not want to, *or could not*—to be precise, based on the determined stare emanating from Anna— get rid of her at that moment.

So, instead of standing there and trying to break up with her during their first encounter, Senn decided he would let her tag along for the trip to the Teatro and see what she knew that could give him some leads into finding Laura.

Looking unconvinced, Senn gave a slightly frustrated sigh and walked past Anna down the street towards the Teatro, half-heartedly hoping she would not follow.

But she did.

"Mr. Senn?" Anna said as she ran and caught up with him.

"Senn, just call me Senn," Senn pleaded as he quickened his pace.

"OK, Senn," Anna said, emphasizing the letter *n* as she said his name. "Did you know that a Venetian merchant built the Teatro Rossi as a gift for his mistress in 1794?"

"No. I did not." As he kept walking, Senn looked at Google maps to get directions, trying not to pay too much attention to Anna, who walked beside him, looking calm and slightly amused at Senn stopping and starting on the street while looking at his phone for precise directions.

Anna, unperturbed, walked alongside, firing questions at him while walking,

"And that Stephan Conti has owned this place since birth thanks to his mother, the Teatro's real owner?"

Senn stopped and studied Anna's animated gestures as she spoke, slightly more interested in what she said. *Sounds like she did some homework on the case*, thought Senn as he struggled with the route to the Teatro.

Senn saw Anna politely extend her hand and gently invert the phone in his hand to indicate the street Senn was about to walk down was in the opposite direction. Senn looked sheepish and said, "Yes, that's better. Thanks."

Pitying Senn's poor map skills, Anna walked ahead and motioned him to follow with a slight smirk and a flick of her eyebrow.

Senn reluctantly put his phone away and let her lead him to the Teatro and try to impress him with her deep insight about the theatre.

CHAPTER 8

THE TEATRO TREMBLES

Senn and Anna stood outside the imposing marble arched, columned facade of the Teatro Rossi and knocked on the giant, lacquered, green mahogany door.

The Teatro sat on the corner of a stark but majestic square, *Campo San Barnaba*, surrounded by sun-bleached multi-colored houses on two sides and opening onto a wide, sunny canal on the west. The place was busy with locals and tourists milling around the restaurants and shops while some jolly gondoliers flirted with American girls, offering them boat tours.

The back of Senn's head had swollen like a Faberge egg. Instead of finding a doctor, which was what he ideally needed to do, Senn looked in his bag for a painkiller to numb the ache. But the pills were missing, probably lost when his bag tore open during the attack. Luckily, he spotted a small pharmacy sign in one of the shop windows.

He asked Anna to hold the vigil while he got some painkillers and bandages.

He swallowed a couple of paracetamols while standing in the pharmacy and ran back in time to see Anna talking to a middle-aged lady at the door. Senn waited for Anna and the woman to finish speaking in Italian for a minute, then Anna turned to Senn and said, "Elvi is the admin manager of the Teatro and will show us around and answer any questions."

Elvi smiled at Senn and said, "Hi, Mr. Senn. Stephan said he'll try to join us if he can."

Senn thanked Elvi and followed her and Anna into the building. The instant he stepped inside, he heard the muffled sound of a woman sobbing.

He felt the sound coming from under the slabs of thick, white marble that covered the ground. The sound was distinct and persistent. The woman's breath trembled as she sobbed. Senn looked at Anna and Elvi, but neither seemed aware of the sobbing.

It happened to him sometimes. He could hear the wail of wandering souls.

Senn bent and pretended to retie his laces to isolate the sound's location, but he kept hearing the distressed intones echoing from under the stones.

Laura was right, Senn surmised. She had indeed encountered the ghost of the Teatro, and now it was his turn to find her.

In that instant, the sobbing ended.

Senn quietly followed Elvi, who led them to the main auditorium while explaining the history of the theatre and all the famous people who had performed or visited the place recently. Anna scribbled furiously into her little moleskin notebook as she listened intently to Elvi's spiel.

They entered the auditorium from one of the stage exit doors, arrived directly on the theatre stage, and peered into the dimly lit, 400-seat oval space. Senn was surprised by the starkness of the decor. Unlike other Venetian theatres that were heavily robed and gilded, this theatre was more frugal.

There were no grand painted ceilings, gold braiding on the walls, or a giant chandelier dangling from the roof. It was an industrial, raw, and semi-finished version of the classical theatres in the city.

Surprised at the spartan look, Senn asked why, and Elvi explained by pointing to a fire extinguisher on the wall, "We had a fire here two years ago that caused a lot of damage to the Teatro. We are slowly building it all back to its past glory."

Anna nodded sympathetically. "But how long have you been closed to the public then?"

Elvi hesitated and said, "We're reopening for the first time after the fire in March."

Senn nodded. This made sense. Laura had joined the theatre six months ago to oversee the restoration, the severity of which Senn had underestimated.

Senn looked carefully at the walls and saw the remnants of old scorched wallpaper still peeling off in some places. How come no one had mentioned that to him?

"And are you going to be ready?" Anna asked, looking worried at the amount of work still pending. Senn, in the meantime, had walked further backstage and tried entering a room but found it locked.

He needed to find the way to the basement.

"Well, we've been practicing hard." Elvi perked up with excitement as she described the hectic rehearsal schedules that Stephan was leading daily but remarked how the disappearance of Laura had made all the cast nervous and slowed the rehearsals.

"Do you have a basement here?" Senn asked with urgency, surprising both women simultaneously.

After a pause, Elvi said, "Yes, but I've never been down there, and frankly, I'm not allowed to go there. Why do you want to go *there*?"

"I've read it still has a medieval crypt. Can you show me the way, please?" Senn asked, making up an excuse on the fly. Elvi hesitated for a second and then, with a shrug, led Senn past a narrow hallway with dressing rooms on either side to a dimly lit alley with a metal door at the end of the passage and stopped and turned to Senn and Anna. "It's down this way. But I'll stay here if you don't mind. I'm warning you, Mr. Senn, Stephan will not be happy to see you go down there."

Senn put his hand into the side of his backpack, pulled out his torch, switched it on, and turned the handle on the old, faded door, which opened with an echoing creak and revealed a set of narrow steps that headed into the musty darkness below. Senn looked for a light switch, but Elvi was unsure where it could be and stepped back and watched Senn and Anna warily from a safe distance.

Senn looked at Anna. "You want to come?"

Anna nodded and was already looking over Senn's shoulder, keen to explore.

Senn turned the dial of his torch head to widen the light to the max and then led the way. After about ten steps, they reached the base of the building. The air had a strong sulfur smell, and Senn spotted some rats scurrying away from the light as he walked onto a large hall about three meters high, supported by concrete pillars and wooden beams spread out around them. The place was stacked with old furniture and upholstery all around. There was also the sound of some water flowing in the distance.

Suddenly, the sobbing sound reappeared.

But this time, it came from a specific location in the far corner of the basement. Senn, frowning and alert, turned to Anna and asked, "Can you hear someone?" Anna shook her head blankly, looking at Senn with some trepidation.

Senn hurried ahead, getting closer to the trembling sobs as they grew louder and louder.

CHAPTER 9

"SHE KILLED ME."

"It is forbidden to kill; therefore all murderers are punished unless they kill in large numbers and to the sound of trumpets."

—VOLTAIRE

Senn dashed towards the sound of the sobbing woman, with Anna right behind him as they dodged through burnt furniture and musty stage props.

About a hundred meters into the dank space, his torchlight spotted a bulky, charred door leaning against the wall in front of them. Senn could hear the sobs coming directly from behind this door.

Senn motioned to Anna with his finger to stay quiet. Anna was panting and looked perplexed by Senn's mysterious beeline move toward the pile of junk in an otherwise desolate junkyard.

Senn could feel something standing on his left, pointing at a pile of dusty, grey tarpaulin behind the door, covering some tall objects. Senn reached out to touch the cover when he heard a woman whisper, *"Lei mi ha ucciso."*

Senn was stunned. The voice had just whispered: *she killed me.*

Senn turned to see a scared and confused Anna. Unable to hold back her frustration, she blurted out, "What's going on, Senn? I'm scared."

Senn knew he was alarming the young woman with his zombied actions. She had no clue what he had heard or what led him to this spot. He had to quickly make up some excuse to stay and investigate the place longer.

Senn smiled at Anna calmly and said, "Sorry, my fault. I thought I heard some movement in this section. But it was just some bats." Senn said, pointing to a hanging bat up in the ceiling.

Anna did not like his answer. It made it even worse as her eyes widened further and her face clearly said she wanted to leave.

But Senn *had* to see what was behind that tarpaulin.

In the back of Senn's mind, there was the constant whirring hope that he would discover a passage or secret door that might point to the kidnappers' route to smuggle out Laura.

At that moment, a dozen tungsten lights lit up the basement like a basketball court, shattering the impasse, and

Stephan's frantic voice called Senn's name in the distance. Senn shot Anna a glance; she looked visibly relieved.

Sensing there wasn't much time, Senn walked up to the cover and pulled it off with a quick flick, revealing a giant stage mirror and some old desks and props clustered in front. Senn poked his head behind the props to see if there was a hidden exit but saw nothing.

Senn pulled back and stared hard at the objects, unable to find something meaningful, until he spotted a painted canvas behind some large suitcases.

Senn could see Stephan striding fast toward him in a flowing gown, looking annoyed and calling his name repeatedly, asking him to stop removing the covers.

"Mr. Senn. Please stop! Please! Stop doing what you are doing!" Stephan's steely voice shot out like a flying knife as Senn managed to pull the large painting out of the furniture pile.

Stephan rushed past Anna, grabbed the painting out of Senn's hands, and shouted, "Mr. Senn, please stop!" Stephan's face was red and sweaty as he held the canvas away from Senn.

Senn could not understand why Stephan was getting so agitated by his actions. Yes, he knew he was trespassing and poking around his basement, but the dusty painting was getting more drama out of Stephan than expected.

"Sorry, Stephan. I was just admiring all the treasures you have stored here."

"Mr. Senn, I thought you wanted to see the Teatro as normal people do, not like a sneaking rat!" Stephan sneered.

Unperturbed by the insult, Senn kept his eyes on Stephan and then moved it down to the painting in his hand. "C'mon, my friend, I just decided to start at the bottom and make my way to the top. And I'm glad I did; see, I found this fabulous painting. Is it a prop for one of your productions?

In his mind, Senn wanted to know if Laura had chanced upon the painting and triggered a deluge of problems for herself.

Stephan looked down at the painting and, with a shrug, replied, "Yes, it belongs to my mother. All this stuff used to be in her green room when she was an actress." Regaining his belligerence, Stephan glared at Senn and said, "I think you need to leave now."

Senn lowered his eyes and pretended to reason with Stephan while staring at the painting. In the mirror's reflection, he saw the image Stephan was trying to hide.

It showed the long, sad face of a young Italian woman dressed in a low-neck, red velvet embroidered evening gown with frizzy, dark hair, sitting on a table with a drink in her hand.

Senn looked up at Stephan, saw Anna in the mirror behind him looking extremely embarrassed and uncomfortable, and said, "OK, Stephan. We'll leave. I'm sorry if this bothered you so much. I just wondered if Laura had seen this painting."

Stephan shook his head and replied, "Not to my knowledge. We never discussed it."

Stephan put the painting down and turned it so Senn could see it. Still not completely satisfied, Senn remarked in a gushing tone, "Beautiful painting, though! Is this your mother when she was an actress?"

Senn *had to* know who this woman was.

After a long pause, Stephan replied quietly, "No. It's my grandmother."

CHAPTER 10

"YOU'RE MAKING ME UNCOMFORTABLE."

Anna stormed out of the Teatro Rossi, fuming at Senn, who followed quietly, albeit hiding his excruciating aches. His head was throbbing from the mugger's bludgeoning a few hours ago, and his bones ached from experiencing the ghost.

Stephan was hiding something sinister about the basement and the painting he had unearthed. The wailing ghost of the Teatro had stopped crying the moment Senn had pulled the canvas out.

The painting itself was ordinary, but the revelation that it belonged to Stephan's grandmother surprised Senn. Was the ghost suggesting Stephan's grandmother was a killer? Who was Stephan's grandmother? He had to get to the bottom of that one fast.

Stephan's level of rage also unsettled Senn. This innocuous little pile was precious to Stephan in a sprawling basement full of broken, burnt junk. While all these questions swam like little sharks around his head, Senn spotted the bobbing head of an angry Anna trying to get his attention.

Senn had a bad habit. He tended to zone out on everything while concentrating, and Anna was his latest victim. Senn returned to the present and focused on Anna's wrinkled, crabbed face, sitting across him in a busy Trattoria, holding a menu card and saying something to him.

"Sorry, could you repeat that?" Senn said apologetically.

"I said, what the hell just happened there!?" Anna replied, looking exasperated. "I mean, you just ran around the basement like a maniac pulling out paintings and pissing off one of our key witnesses. We'll never be allowed to enter the place again, Senn!"

Senn lowered his gaze, feeling guilty for Anna's well-meaning trepidations. They'd only met a few hours ago but had already shared some wild encounters. Even though he didn't think she was the right person to assist him in this search for Laura, he felt it was time to level with her.

"Sorry, Anna, I need to clarify some things," said Senn.

He told her about the ghost in the Teatro and how Laura had seen it just before she disappeared and mentioned it to Stephan, who had, in turn, told Senn.

"So, did you see the ghost?" Anna cut Senn short as he tried to elaborate on his suspicions about Stephan.

"No, but I felt something guide me to the painting."

Senn lied, as usual, about his psychic powers.

Senn never told anyone about his *paranormal disease,* as he referred to it himself. His bitter-sweet *soul flashes.*

It was his clandestine enigma with which he had a lifelong love-hate relationship. He resented how the power *used him* to express itself. It was like an alien force that forcibly penetrated his body and indulged its omniscient muscles for a while, leaving him ravaged after cashing in its supernatural chips.

Senn never felt he had any control over the power.

It flashed itself alive, revealing some (oftentimes a dark, sinister) secret in the world, and then abandoned his body, leaving him wracked by unbearable physical and mental anguish.

But Senn was patient and sympathetic to it as well. He knew it was a benevolent spirit driven by compassion and not deceit, and despite all the grumbling and cowering, he felt it an honor to be its conduit.

Anna looked perplexed and muttered, "Senn, you're making me uncomfortable."

Aware of his response's spookiness, Senn leaned back, raised his hands in the air. "I'm sorry, Anna. It's weird as hell, I know. But it's just how I felt down there. I was shit scared, but I had to try it to help find Laura."

Senn's disarming voice and surrendered gesture had a domino effect on Anna. After a long, hollow stare, she sighed and slumped in her chair, resting her head on the table, relaxing in his presence for the first time since meeting him in the dingy alleyway.

Senn smiled at Anna and said, "You were brave down there."

With a grin, Anna raised her head and replied, "How's your head?"

Senn cupped his palm over the Faberge bump on his head and cheekily proclaimed, "It kicks hard. I think it's a boy."

Then in a sober tone said, "This is now the second person who's told me to get out of the Teatro. The first was the fake priest who sermoned me with a club and told me to stay away from the Teatro."

Anna's eyes widened. "Is that what he said?"

Senn popped another painkiller as he nodded at Anna.

Anna went silent as she took out her phone, flicked through something, and then came to a stop and turned the phone to show the picture. Senn leaned forward and was surprised that the mugger on the boat in his priest costume was standing a few feet away from Senn.

Before Senn could say anything, Anna sheepishly said, "I was just getting to know you better, but from a distance, Senn."

Before Anna could take the phone back, Senn grabbed it and zoomed into the photograph until it showed the back of the man's hand and a diffused impression of the tattoo Senn had seen.

It was as Senn had imagined—a black double-wing.

Senn gave Anna the zoomed picture and asked, "The guy had this tattoo on his hands. Does it mean anything to you?"

Anna stared at the tattoo for a few seconds in silence and then replied in a grim tone, "It's the symbol of the Mafia Veneta, the local mafia in Venice." After a pause, she continued, "They operate all over the city committing money laundering and extortion, but the major source of their income is trading drugs."

Senn looked at the tattoo carefully, glanced up at a concerned-looking Anna, and said, "So why does the Venetian mafia have a problem with me visiting the Teatro? And what did Laura do that could have pissed them off?"

Laura might be mixed up with the mafia.

CHAPTER 11

"THERE'S SOMETHING STRANGE ABOUT MIA."

"Hearing nuns' confessions is like
being stoned to death with popcorn."

—FULTON J. SHEEN

When his phone rang, Anna and Senn sat in the sunny, boisterous Venetian square, brooding about the link between Laura and the Venetian mafia. Unsure of the caller, Senn answered.

"Mr. Senn? It's Mia, Stephan's mama. I am sorry to disturb you, but I need to see you urgently. I have found some things in my boat that I wish to show you immediately."

Senn was taken aback by Mia's soft, wispy voice, almost pleading to see him. Senn detected a distinct nervousness in her voice, unlike the serene, pious lady he had met earlier this morning.

Anna pursed her lips and creased her eyebrows when Senn signaled it was Mia on the phone.

"Sure, madam, I can come there right away. Where's your boat?" Senn asked as he got ready to locate her on Google.

"It's at the Darsena Croze in San Zorzi Mazor. I am at the clubhouse just opposite the harbor. If you get here in an hour, I can show you myself, and we can talk about a few other things." Before Senn could ask anything else, Mia apologized for an incoming call she had to take and hung up.

Senn suspected that Stephan had called Mia and tattled about their misadventure at the Teatro. Otherwise, why would she want to see him about *a few other things?*

For the first time, Senn felt that Mia was hiding something about Laura. He looked up to tell Anna about the appointment but noticed she was feverishly scribbling something in her pocket notebook like a nerdy student. She kept her head down and mumbled, "*scusi, solo un attimo.*"

"Sure, take your time," replied Senn as he checked Google for the route to the harbor from their Teatro square.

He'd been there once. It was on the island of San Giorgio Maggiore overlooking the famous St. Marco square. Senn visited the island with Laura a few summers ago and enjoyed the stunning views of Venice from the church bell tower.

Anna tucked her notebook into her backpack and nodded in agreement about heading to meet Mia. She warmly smiled at Senn as she tied back her shoulder-length, dark, wavy hair and said, "Sorry, I had to make a few notes about Mia calling you just a few minutes after we came out of the Teatro. Have you met her? I have, and frankly, I find her a bit scary. She's the owner of the Teatro, as I mentioned earlier, but the more I dig into her past, the stranger she sounds!"

Anna talked animatedly as she and Senn walked towards the Rezzonico ferry stop to catch the Vaporetto until Giglio. From there, they had to walk for two kilometers until they reached the San Marco ferry, crossed over to the island stop of San Giorgio, and the harbor and the boat were a few minutes from there.

Senn was intrigued by Anna's assessment of Mia. Senn had not caught any strangeness in Mia when they had met and thus was curious about Anna's perspective.

"Tell me what's so strange about Mia," Senn asked.

Anna looked gingerly at Senn's intense stare and said, "I'll tell you what I think, but I can't prove all of it, OK?"

Senn nodded, encouraging her to speak her mind.

Looking a bit reassured, Anna began, "So, remember Stephan mentioned Mia was an actress when she was young? Well, I also thought so when I first read about this case. So I checked the register of the Venetian artists guild. But I couldn't find any mention of her name. Then when I checked her mother's name, Luigina Conti, it showed up, and the records state that she is still alive since 1932." Anna paused and said, "That's about 90 years ago."

The Vaporetto they had boarded a few minutes ago at Rezzonico reached Giglio, where they had to get off.

Senn started to reply but second-guessed himself, so Anna continued. "Yes, I thought, OK, no big deal." Anna's eyes narrowed. "But when I checked Luigina Conti's history, I found something odd. Luigina Conti died while giving birth to a baby girl named Mia in 1962."

Anna jumped off the boat first and put her hand out to help Senn off.

Senn had a blinding soul flash when he held Anna's hand.

He saw a hooded man with a bloodied knife rushing toward her. Senn could feel his blazing hate glowing around his body as he bounded towards Anna.

The flash froze Senn in his tracks. The man resembled the mugger who had just attacked him. Anna, lost in her Mia story, hardly noticed Senn's jolted demeanor as she scurried ahead, eager to continue her bizarre suspicions about Mia.

Senn was in turmoil. He couldn't make sense of what the flash meant. What was the connection between Anna and the mugger? And why was he attacking Anna?

And then it struck him.

The mafia had added Anna to their list of threats because they saw she was cooperating with him. The soul flash was warning him about an imminent assault on her and also confirming Laura's disappearance was linked to the mafia.

Senn suddenly felt a kinship with Anna. In that instant, he changed his mind and decided she would be his partner in finding Laura.

Happy with his decision, Senn redirected his attention to Anna to complete her Mia story.

Anna's grey eyes darkened, and she said, "Senn, Mia is the most private person I've ever met. I've no way of proving she is who she says she is. She could be an imposter."

"What?" Senn asked, not sure what Anna was implying.

Anna held his elbow, shook it, and pleaded, "I know it makes no sense. But hear me out, Senn. I've checked. The only record I have come across is that she owns the Teatro. No childhood, no husband. No siblings. Nothing. Nobody knows Stephan's father, and Stephan has never explained that to anyone. Both mother and son hold that secret close to their chest."

Senn shrugged, unconvinced. "Mia could be a private person and worked under her mother's moniker. I don't see that as a reason to suspect her."

They had reached the crowded San Marco ferry stop, and the glistening island of San Giorgio Maggiore, with its majestic marble columns and stoic bell tower, loomed in the distance.

CHAPTER 12

"THIS BELONGS TO LAURA!"

"Hope is the thing with feathers that perches in the soul and sings the tune without the words. And never stops at all."

—EMILY DICKINSON

Senn paced the cold, bare promenade of the San Marco ferry station, smoldering in self-doubt.

He'd been in Venice for over a day and had not made any meaningful headway toward finding Laura. It had already been five days and seven hours since she went missing. He'd regularly checked all social media accounts, but nothing had surfaced. Her phone was off and going straight to voicemail.

The police had not come up with any fresh leads either.

Senn had met with every neighbor in the building, and no one had seen or heard anything untoward. Most of Laura's neighbors were women who worked in the theatre district and did not know each other too well, including Laura. The place was like a hostel with many short-stay tenants who came and left without building meaningful bonds with each other.

The frustration worsened for him last night when he spoke to Laura's distraught parents and tried to bolster their sagging hopes and distract them from imagining the worst.

Becoming a target of the Venetian mafia and being led to a veiled painting in the Teatro basement felt like insidious clues in a bottomless whirlpool. He desperately needed something tangible to light his path to Laura.

Sitting on the mooring bollard dangling her legs, Anna turned to Senn and asked, "What's wrong?"

Still adrift in his fog of doubt, Senn mumbled, "The Vaporetto's taking too long."

Anna squinted into the setting sun, pointed at the approaching boat, and said, "It's here."

Senn was the first to step on the boat. He was eager to see what Mia had found, yet wary of her motives.

As discovered by Anna, the lack of any tangible personal history stirred his doubts about her character and motives. It was also surprising how eager she was to share new, vital information about Laura with him directly vs. dealing first with the police. Was it a genuine attempt to aid the investigation or a ploy to engender trust? Mia was Stephan's only alibi on the night Laura disappeared. Was she protecting him from being the prime suspect?

All these questions added foliage to her shrouded mottle-tailed image in his mind.

Senn sighted the string of moored boats in the harbor from the open deck of the Vaporetto as it approached the San Giorgia landing spot. As they walked up to the harbor entrance, Senn recognized Mia sitting alone on a crimson chaise-longue, peering expectantly from behind the large, oval glass windows of the clubhouse.

Mia stood, waved at Senn, and signaled him to come in from the main stanchioned red-carpet entrance. After logging their identities in a cyclopean leather register, the polite uniformed receptionist at the door escorted them to Mia.

Mia appeared sedate in her peach embroidered dress as she shook Senn's hands and waited for him to introduce Anna to her. Her almost-empty glass of white wine and a wrinkled tissue under the table were the only signs of her feeling of discomposure.

Mia greeted Anna with a courteous smile and grasped her outstretched hand in a shake. Then she turned to Senn and said with a deep sigh, "I'm so glad you're both here. I didn't know what to do with the thing I found in the boat this morning, so I thought I'd first call you."

Pointing to the harbor, she continued in a slightly flustered tone, "Mr. Senn, I normally rent my boat to the club on days I am not using it, and they clean it before they return it to me. But this morning, they found this while they were cleaning. I'm sorry, but I looked inside. I think it's Laura's."

Mia took a small, red leather wallet from her bag and handed it to Senn. Senn's eyes widened with excitement as he asked Mia to place the wallet on the table while he pulled out his forensic gloves.

Senn's pulse raced as he picked up the wallet and looked for any signs of damage or blood. "Where did you find these?" Senn carefully removed its contents and placed them on the table.

"My cleaners found them behind the leather seats in the cabin," Mia replied, now sounding nervous. "Oh, God! I hope I didn't mess up things by touching it," Mia said as she watched Senn examine the wallet in minute detail.

It *was* Laura's wallet.

It had her Italian resident ID card, driving license, bank card, and a photograph of her posing at the Eifel tower. Senn had taken the picture.

Senn looked up at Mia and said in a shaky voice, "It's Laura's."

Anna stood behind Senn solemnly, taking pictures of the wallet and its contents as Mia silently gulped down the last sip of her wine.

Senn held the wallet and hoped for a soul flash to help uncover what had happened to Laura.

Nothing.

Senn replaced the wallet's contents, packed it into a new plastic bag, and put it in his backpack.

Senn was excited nonetheless with the find.

Laura had been in the boat forcibly or unaware. But Senn was surprised that Mia readily gave them such vital evidence. If she were guilty, she would have hidden this from everyone. But he still had to ask her why she came to him first.

Mia looked nervous but quickly regained her poise and said, "Stephan asked me to call you first. So I did."

Stephan was being quite erratic for sure. On the one hand, he tells his mother to share vital information like this first with him and, on the other hand, banishes him unceremoniously from the Teatro.

"We'll take this to the police, madam, and ask them to run some tests on it to see if we can find some DNA or prints." Mia nodded in agreement. Senn then looked at the harbor and asked Mia if they could check the boat.

Senn was a bit surprised by the find. If Laura'd been forced, it was improbable her wallet would have been on her. Wallets tended to be in women's bags that they pack before moving.

As they walked out on the harbor, the creamy green water of Venice exaggerated the fine details of the handsome boat like a felt pad at Tiffany's. The gleaming mahogany speed boat had a distinctive indigo cabin with a gold stripe running down the hull with a wine-red quilted leather couch, a TV, surround sound systems, and a small refrigerator to round off its luxury.

The cabin was large enough for four to six people to sit inside but not enough space to sleep. The cabin door opened to the stern with enough room for a couple to squeeze together. It was a luxury version of a typical water limousine that drove around the city, ferrying tourists to the airport or boat tours around the canals and surrounding islands.

Mia pointed to the corner behind the couch and said, "My cleaners said they remove the seats sometimes to clean under them, and that's how they found the wallet."

Senn inspected the seats and found nothing peculiar. Senn sat and tried to fathom what had happened to Laura in this cabin.

He also made a mental note to find out who rented the boat the night she went missing.

CHAPTER 13

THE MASTERPIECE MOTIVE

"We are all selfish and I no more trust myself than others with a good motive."

—LORD BYRON

Senn goggled at Mia's speed boat's mahogany and leather interiors, pondering how Laura's wallet could have surfaced there.

Mia sat across him on the opposite side, talking to Anna, who quietly scribbled away, listening to her explain how she and Stephan used the boat infrequently.

Mia sounded nervous as she talked. "I was shocked when they brought the wallet to me. Initially, I thought it belonged to some tourist and was about to hand it over to the club that manages the rental arrangements."

Senn interrupted her and asked, "Do you often get lost property brought to you?"

Mia shook her head. "Not that often, and only if they think it's valuable or unusual."

"Who's *they?*" Senn asked.

"Silvio, the club manager," Mia replied, sounding defensive.

Anna raised her head from her notebook and asked, "Can we speak to him?"

Mia nodded and stepped out on the gangway to find him.

Mia had called the police after calling them, so Senn did not have much time to investigate the cabin himself. He looked at the leather seats again.

The seats fitted snugly into the edge with no gaps, and the top of the chairs had a small flap for storing things that ran the entire perimeter of the seats.

Mia said the cleaners had found the wallet behind the seats. Senn found this highly improbable, as there was no space *behind* the seats. A wallet like Laura's could slip inside the storage flaps but not behind. Then Senn looked closely at the edge of the chairs and noticed some clips could unlatch the seat to remove it.

Senn pulled the seat, and the base slid out, revealing a hollow chamber. It was wide enough for a slender/ short person to lie inside. Laura could have easily been concealed here and ferried across. But she would have to be sedated to lie here without making a scene.

The discovery excited and disturbed Senn in the same breath.

Anna stood behind Senn and, sounding apprehensive, said, "Do you think Laura was in this compartment?"

Senn removed the second seat and replied, "Maybe." He looked up at Anna. "Do you mind lying inside for me to check if she would have fit? She was about your size and height."

Anna stepped in and lay down inside the hollow space. She fitted snugly.

Anna kept lying in the cavity and said, "They could only do this late at night. The smugglers could have posed as tourists. Boats like this operate all night as taxis ferrying passengers from the airport, and I saw this boat has a taxi license."

Senn shook his head, unsure of Anna's theory. "But surely people would have seen a sedated woman being carted onto a boat? I think they moved her from private docks." After a pause, Senn added, "Does the Teatro have a private dock? We need to check that immediately."

The cabin door opened, and Mia walked in with a middle-aged burly bald man in tow. She froze at the sight of Anna lying inside the hollowed seat.

"Oh my God!" Mia shrieked, raising her hands to her face. "Is this where they kept the girl? Shocking! How shocking! Mr. Senn, is that what you think?"

Senn didn't answer but helped Anna out of her seat. He signaled at the leather chairs and said, "It's one possibility, but we can't be sure. The police will have to check for DNA and see if they find anything."

He turned his attention to the man Mia had brought with her. Mia introduced him as Silvio, the travel manager, who smiled warmly and shook their hands.

Silvio dressed in a three-piece, long-tail black tuxedo with the club emblem embroidered in gold on his lapel. He spoke softly with a thick Italian accent. "I check with the cleaners, and they confirm to me also that the wallet was under the seat in this area."

Senn nodded. "Did they find anything else?"

Silvio shook his head. "No. It was everything."

Senn continued, "How often do they clean under the seats?"

"One time per month," replied Silvio.

Senn turned to Mia and asked, "What do you normally use this place for? It looks almost brand new."

Mia, looking baffled, replied, "Frankly, I had forgotten we have this space, Mr. Senn. We use the boat sometimes when we have to pick up guests from the airport or when I go to our beach house."

Senn raised his eyebrow. "And where's your beach house, madam?"

"In Malamocco, on Lido Island," Mia replied, looking a little tired by all the excitement of discovering Laura's wallet.

"So, when was the last time you used the boat?" Senn asked as he replaced the seats.

"Well, this morning!" Mia replied, raising her voice over the passing speedboats in the lagoon. "I picked up the boat early this morning with the skipper from here and went to pick up Stephan to take him shopping for a party we're hosting tonight at the beach house. Then I dropped him off at the Teatro and returned to the club to have lunch. That's when Silvio brought the wallet to me, and I decided to call you before informing the police."

Senn helped Mia off the boat and continued, "Did Stephan tell you we were at the Teatro today?"

Mia looked surprised and replied, "No, not yet, but I suppose he'll tell me later when we meet. Did you find something there?"

Senn glanced at Anna and noticed her penetrating eyes tearing into Mia's gestures and body language as she spoke.

Senn was curious how she would react to his following statement as he dropped his gaze and casually remarked, "We found your mother's painting."

Mia stiffened and looked at him with a smile. “Oh God! Did you? Where?! Stephan said it got burnt in the fire.”

Senn looked at Anna and then back at Mia. “Stephan had it safely in the basement.”

Mia, visibly moved by the news and with a loud sigh of relief, said, “How wonderful. You know the painting was a gift to my mother by Modigliani.”

Senn’s eyes widened as he hesitantly asked, “Amedeo Modigliani?”

“Yes, they were lovers,” Mia replied with pride.

CHAPTER 14

PERDONAMI PADRE

"But in the end, one needs more courage to live than to kill himself."

—ALBERT CAMUS

Silvio was frowning as he walked up to Senn and announced, "Sir, we can't make contact with Captain Luca. He is not answering his phone."

Silvio had called the taxi union and found out who was driving Mia's boat the night Laura disappeared. The captain's name was Luca Bonato, a seasoned captain in the Venetian lagoon and Silvio's friend.

Silvio seemed agitated as he continued spluttering, saying it was unusual for Luca not to pick up the phone. He had taken the day off yesterday by reporting sick. Silvio tried to call a few others, and no one had heard from Luca for more than a day. His neighbor had seen a lock on his front door and thought he was visiting his daughter, who lived in Rome. Silvio looked rattled. According to him, Luca had no plans of going on holiday, so the locked front door was unusual.

Senn offered to check on Luca at his home. Anna agreed and asked Silvio, who arranged for a taxi to ferry them to his flat in St. Elena and promised to follow an hour after his shift ended.

St. Elena was 10 minutes away and gave Senn a few minutes to assess the situation.

He was still recovering from the shocking admission from Mia that the painting was an original Modigliani. Paintings by this artist were worth millions, and the fact that Mia's grandmother was his lover made the news even more scandalous. And why had Stephan lied to his mother about the loss of the painting? Surely it was insured.

Someone was lying.

He stood on the deck and zipped up his jacket as the wind brought the ocean's cold front into the canals. Anna smiled at Senn and said, "What a day, huh?"

"Yeah, but it's not over," Senn replied with a sigh.

Anna bit her lip nervously. "I hope he's OK."

Senn was curious about what Anna thought of Mia after this meeting. "Do you believe her?" he asked.

Anna looked back at Senn through her windswept hair. "I know she's lying about some things. I don't know how many. She and Stephan are very close, Senn, so I don't believe she didn't know that the painting was in the basement."

"And what about the wallet?" Senn continued

Anna puckered her lips and shook her head, not convinced. "She could have easily put it there and called us to seem innocent."

Senn shrugged and, prepared to get off the boat, replied, "It's possible. We can clear some of that if we speak to the Captain."

The boat lined up a few meters ahead of the St Elena ferry stop, and Anna jumped off and led the way in locating Luca's house in the cramped alleyway a few hundred meters inland. They reached a runty grey padlocked door at the dim street corner with laundry hanging outside on drooping clotheslines fluttering in the wind.

"Is there a back door?" Senn asked as he tested the padlock that looked weathered but secure.

Anna circuited around the sides and walked onto the thin service ledge that abutted the waterway. Senn followed until they came face-to-face with a rusted metal door with a white spot-painted handle. Next to it was an old, foul-smelling garbage bin stapled to the wall with some fading cord around it. Senn tried the handle, and to their surprise, it turned, and the door opened with a faint creaking sound.

Narrow steps led directly to the floor above. At the end of the stairs was another small, wooden door that was ajar with a floor rug slightly sticking out. The lights were off in the flat as Senn pushed the door open.

He gave a loud gasp and grimaced at what he saw.

The body of a lifeless man hung from the wooden crossbeam in the room.

Senn's reaction rippled down to Anna, who froze on the steps, visibly shaken and afraid. He pulled out his torch and entered, and Anna followed gingerly and muffled a scream on seeing the hanging corpse.

The man's bent head with his long, grey hair obstructed a clear view of his face. The white nylon rope around the neck hung from a wooden crossbeam a few feet above him and occasionally made an eerie creaking sound due to the wind outside. An old kitchen stool lay on the floor under the corpse. His skin had turned purple, and his face bloated with eyes bulging. He wore a faded blue nightgown, an old vest, and pyjamas. Senn could tell from the rigor mortis that he'd been dead for almost 24 hours.

Anna found a light switch on the wall and turned on the lights.

It was hard for Senn to walk around the body without bumping into the old furniture in the crowded room. Was the hanging body that of Luca? He scanned the pictures on the wall while slapping on his gloves to make sure. He could see many framed photographs of Luca with his long, grey ponytail, smiling and laughing with a woman and a little girl. Senn grudgingly surmised the body did look like it was Luca.

They had to hurry. In a few minutes, they needed to call the police.

Senn touched the radiators and found them cold. He took out his phone and started taking pictures without touching anything.

In the meantime, Anna, who had walked into the bathroom, let out a shocked scream. Senn rushed in and stared at the mirror.

Scrawled across the mirror in white toothpaste were the words *Perdonami Padre.*

Senn, taken aback, looked at Anna in the mirror, who grimly translated, "Forgive me, Father." After a pause, she whispered, "Looks like the poor guy hung himself."

How odd, thought Senn.

Except for the *last-minute* suicide scrawl, the place was meticulous and spotless.

The bedsheets stretched, the kitchen sink shining, no newspapers or magazines strewn around except the heavily stickered fridge.

Inside, the refrigerator lay stuffed with half-empty beer cans, leftover pizzas, dirty plastic bags, and wilting vegetables. It looked like Luca had swept the place for hours (except the refrigerator) before hanging himself.

To Senn, it seemed highly suspicious that the same Luca who kept his refrigerator like a pigsty would dry clean his apartment before calling it quits. Either Luca developed schizophrenia on his last day, or someone had carefully staged his death after strangling him.

Senn looked in the trash can for the toothpaste tube used to write on the mirror and found nothing. Pointing out that omission, Senn commented, "If I were going to use toothpaste to sign my suicide note, I would throw the empty tube in the bin. But Luca didn't."

Anna nodded. "Whoever made it look like suicide was not trying too hard to hide it. It's more like they were trying to mock him while covering their tracks."

Senn paused and exclaimed, "Precisely! The killer had a macabre sense of humor."

Senn pointed his flashlight at the kitchen wall and noticed something strange. Hidden behind a stack of half-empty sauce and ketchup bottles was a small key holder on the wall with a single key with the Teatro Rossi insignia keychain. Senn took out the key and put it in his pocket. He needed to find the lock that opened this key.

He had a hunch the killer was looking for this key.

CHAPTER 15

UNTYING THE KNOTS OF MAYHEM

"If I cease searching, then, woe is me, I am lost. That is how I look at it — keep going, keep going, come what may."

—VINCENT VAN GOGH

Senn lay sleepless in bed, gazing at the exposed wooden beams of the attic, holding the Teatro Rossi keychain, trying to unwrap the motives of each of the characters he'd encountered so far.

Starting with Stephan Conti, the saturnine director of the Teatro Rossi and one of the prime suspects in Senn's eyes. The tortured soul and devoted son came across as someone who tossed uncontrollably between theatrical brilliance and deep bouts of self-despair. It was hard to peer through the permanent mask of fret that tainted all his thoughts and actions.

He was the last person who'd spoken to Laura before she disappeared. His motive was straightforward. He wanted to conceal what she had uncovered in the Teatro. She'd told Stephan she'd seen a ghost there who wept about being murdered in the Teatro. *What else had Laura found that he was concealing?*

The ghost had led Senn to the basement and showed him her killer by revealing the painting. Stephan again had desperately tried to conceal its presence from Senn and Anna. It was a painting by Modigliani of Mia's great-grandmother that made it a valuable family heirloom.

Had Laura found damning clues in the family history proving this crime and confronted Stephan?

The discovery of Laura's wallet in their boat was also incriminating evidence against Stephan. He could have lured the unsuspecting girl on a trip before forcibly abducting her with Luca's help.

Senn suspected Stephan ordered Luca's killing as well. He was paranoid that the captain might rat on him under pressure and therefore paid someone to get rid of him. Stephan seemed too sophisticated to carry out the killing himself. Senn suspected someone more professional did the dirty work.

Which brought Senn to his true enigma. The ephemeral Mia.

Anna was partially right about the elusiveness of Mia's personal history. Senn had carried out his checks through public records and found very little information about her except while tracing the chain of owners of the Teatro Rossi.

The Teatro's publicly accessible ownership records dated back to 1904 to a woman called Perina Zambin, an actress and wife of a wine merchant who had bought the Teatro and gifted it to his wife.

Senn dug further into Perina's history and found that she was indeed acquainted with Modigliani and frequented cafes and nightclubs in Venice from 1905 to 06. She supposedly was the woman who introduced him to hashish. Some art historians had found letters between Modigliani and Perina that suggested she was pregnant with his child when he decided to leave Venice and move to Paris for good.

Perina gave birth to Emilia in 1906 and passed the ownership of the Teatro to her when she turned 18 in 1924.

Emilia married a famous tenor in the Venetian opera, Carlo Gigli, who brought a lot of fame and glamor to the Teatro with his performances and social circle of friends.

After many miscarriages, Emilia gave birth to Luigina on 2nd July 1942. The family was ecstatic! But tragedy struck again when, just a day after giving birth to Luigina, Emilia suddenly passed away due to a massive heart attack. Carlo was distraught and died in despair by drowning in the canal outside the Teatro.

Luigina was raised by her mother-in-law, Sophie. She was a well-respected shamanic healer in Venice and often traveled to Africa and India on healing missions to meet her gurus. Luigina met her husband, Major Claudio Conti, on one of these missions when she turned 18.

The public records became sketchy after this. But Senn discovered a memoir of the major of his travels in India where he found some more tantalizing details of his life with Luigina.

The major was a well-respected Italian surgeon stationed in India, helping inoculate the country's children against smallpox and Polio. It was love at first sight for both of them, and they got married in Rajasthan. But death was the uninvited guest at their wedding when Sophie died the same night in her sleep, a victim of a deadly rattlesnake bite.

To distract Luigina from the grief of losing her foster mother, the major took a year's sabbatical from the army and took his young bride on a twelve-month adventure around Asia.

Unfortunately, the trip ended in disaster when the major suddenly developed a high fever and passed away while in Shanghai. Luigina completed the memoir while returning to Venice, eight months pregnant and in deep depression.

The only record of Mia's birth Senn found was speculation in a newspaper that Mia was born on a cruise liner where her mother died while giving birth to her on the 2nd of July, 1962.

The only record of Mia Conti after that date was while recording the birth of her son Stephan, born July 4th, 1982, twenty years later. Senn could not track any details about Stephan's father/Mia's spouse. All subsequent records show Luigina Conti as the actress performing exclusively in the Teatro Rossi.

From all this digging, Senn was almost sure that Emilia was Modigliani's illegitimate daughter making Mia the great-granddaughter of the legendary artist.

CHAPTER 16

CLUES ALWAYS HIDE THEIR CLAWS

"The darkest hours reveal the most light."

-RUMI

Senn heard loud knocking as he jumped out of bed, still sodden with sleep. It was barely 6 AM.

The crumpled face of the bloated, breathless landlord was at the door. On the floor were three hastily packed bulky brown boxes. In a calm voice, the landlord pointed to the boxes and said, "I have to give these to you." Before Senn could inquire about their contents, the man pushed the boxes into the studio and said, "It's your friend's stuff. I need to empty the flat."

Sounding irritated, he said, "She missed her rent last month, and who knows where she is now. I have two ex-wives and three children to feed, sir. I can't wait any longer."

Senn, surprised Laura had missed her rent, tried to resist, but the man turned and walked down the stairs saying he was sorry, but it was just business, nothing personal.

Senn closed the door while rubbing his neck and head, still sore from the mugging a few days ago. A cursory look suggested the boxes contained a mix of clothes, shoes, books, photographs, and some wall hangings. He took them out and laid them on the dining table to get a quick overview. The police had completed the search of her flat and did not come up with anything concrete.

A lump rose in Senn's throat as he gently dusted the photo frames of a beaming, tanned Laura backpacking around the world that used to hang on her wall. The books were primarily novels and her art history books. He didn't find any diaries that could give him clues to her state of mind in the last few weeks before she vanished.

He desperately wanted to find her alive and healthy.

Senn was about to close the boxes when he noticed a familiar object stashed at the bottom of one. Her faded, favorite North Face backpack had accompanied her on many trips they had done together. But now it was too frayed and old and had been gracefully retired. Senn took it out and smiled at its age and how it reminded him of Laura's wild, adventurous spirit. He checked all the pockets until he felt something hard in one.

Senn unzipped the pocket and pulled out a small, silver jewelry box with an engraved Teatro Rossi emblem. Curious, he opened it and found a silver key inside a groove. Next to it was another slot for a key, which was empty. Senn turned the box over and saw engraved letters and numbers.

Senn stared at it and tried to make sense of the numbers.

667212345AQ

A shiver of recognition went down his spine.

It was a laser-cut platinum key to unlock sophisticated Swiss Bank safety deposit boxes.

Senn had read about these legendary keys because the safety boxes they operated were supposed to be impregnable and could only open if used simultaneously after inputting each key's unique account number.

The Teatro Rossi emblem on top suggested it was the property of Mia and Stephan. The shocking thing was that Laura had one key.

Senn was intrigued by this find. Why did Laura have something so valuable to the Conti family?

Was this the reason for her mysterious disappearance?

Senn added the key to his keychain, took a picture of the account number, and hid the box in the bag.

If this key was the only hope for Laura's life, then Senn intended to guard it with his life.

Senn hurriedly got ready to meet Anna for breakfast at Campo, eager to share this discovery with her.

Thanks to her uncle, she'd gotten a copy of the DNA tests conducted on Mia's boat and the autopsy on Luca from the police.

Finally, they could start getting some answers.

Anna had become a trusted ally in the investigation. Senn admired her proactive, meticulous approach, but her steely nature impressed him the most.

It was hard to keep her rattled for too long. Even when she saw the dangling corpse, after the initial shock, she recovered remarkably fast and kept her focus on the investigation without getting emotionally drained. She'd confided to Senn about her dream of becoming a crime detective in Rome, and Senn was confident that she had all the necessary traits to become one.

But they disagreed on one thing: Mia and her motives.

Anna believed Mia had somehow managed to take over the Teatro by getting rid of the real Mia Conti and installing herself and her son, Stephan, into the Teatro. Anna had strong suspicions that Mia was a wandering gypsy who had somehow infiltrated the family and taken over the reins.

Anna's hunch was that Laura had somehow found this out and was threatening to disclose this to the police.

Fearing betrayal, Mia and Stephan plotted and abducted Laura and either disposed of her or were still holding her hostage somewhere and waiting for the right opportunity to kill her once the hype of their search died.

Senn decided to stay open-minded until Anna could prove her suspicions.

When Senn arrived and lightly touched her shoulder, Anna was already engrossed in reading something, sipping her sugarless double expresso head spinner. Anna jerked her head up like an angry feral, not expecting to see Senn so early. Amused by the ferocity, Senn backed off and smiled and apologized for disturbing her. She dropped her shoulders, giggled her apology, and pleaded, "Sennnnn, don't do that!" Senn laughed, punched her a high five, sat down, and warmed his hands with his breath.

Anna kept reading, slid a stack of papers towards him, and said, "They're in Italian, but I think you'll be able to make out its gist quite quickly." Senn could read and understand Italian but was uncomfortable speaking it. He had fresh memories of being mocked for trying.

Senn peered at the DNA test results, and slowly his eyes lit up as he punched the air excitedly. The report confirmed conclusive DNA evidence to prove that Laura *had* been on the boat. They had found hair and saliva (but no blood) in one of the compartments. Senn looked at Anna, psyched, and said, "She was in the boat. That means Luca knew everything about the abduction."

Anna nodded in agreement and sighed. "Yeah, but unfortunately, they couldn't find any foreign DNA in Luca's house. The cause of death in the autopsy report is self-inflicted death by hanging. The guy just cracked under pressure." Senn stood impatiently, took the report from Anna, and read it himself. It declared the cause of death was *asphyxiation due to ligature strangulation,* which was a technical way of saying death by hanging.

Senn *knew* that was false based on his analysis.

Senn suspected Luca knew his killers.

That's why there was no forced entry. Senn suspected his alcohol was spiked from the almost empty bottle of expensive whiskey on the countertop he saw next to cheaper brands of alcohol. And when he became drowsy, he was smothered by a towel or a pillow until he died. The hanging was staged to mislead the police.

Senn read the report until the end, stared blankly at Anna, and said defiantly, "But I know it wasn't suicide."

Anna crossed her arms, leaned back, and narrowed her eyes into slits. But her voice was calm when she asked, "Senn, what's with you? Don't trust the police anymore?

At that instant, Senn decided to return (alone this time) to the flat to find evidence proving his theory and give him additional clues to Laura's whereabouts.

CHAPTER 17

THE TROUBLING LIGHT IN THE TUNNEL

"I wanted movement and not a calm course of existence. I wanted excitement and danger and the chance to sacrifice myself for my love."

—LEO TOLSTOY

It was 2 AM as Senn did a final check of the holstered push dagger around his lower left leg and pulled on his biker boots over them.

He was going back to Luca's house.

Earlier in the day, Senn had tried to convince Anna about his suspicion that someone had murdered Luca and tried to masquerade it as a suicide. He pointed out all the discordant objects in the flat to her. Like the swabbed kitchen sink, the clean bedsheets, pillow covers, and vitally, the lack of fingerprints on the toothpaste tube found in the trash used to write the suicide note.

Senn was vehement that, based on Luca's lengthy police record that Anna had gotten hold of, Luca lived on the wrong side of the law. Luca was a convicted juvenile carjacker, including jail time for burglary, assisted shoplifting, and bootlegging. So in Senn's mind, there was *no real* motive to take such drastic action for a repeat offender like Luca.

Anna disagreed and reminded Senn that Luca suffered from a chronic drinking problem and had a history of fines for driving under the influence. According to the neighbors, he'd recently divorced and was often depressed. And the thing that made him desperate was that the banks were after him to pay his mortgage. He was deep in debt and needed money fast.

In Anna's assessment, he could have aided in Laura's abduction for the money and *maybe even* killed her and then suddenly buckled with remorse and decided to end his life.

Like she said, "The devil caught up with his rotten soul."

Unconvinced, Senn shifted the discussion to the travel logs of the water taxi given to them by the boat club.

The Venetian taxi service GPS logs showed that Luca's boat was busy the night of the abduction, the 4th of February. It had been around the Teatro, dropping off some tourists around midnight, then moved around in the area for an hour, making stops at various hotels and hot spots around Venice. Then between 1–3 AM, the boat's GPS had been switched off at a location on the canal outside the Teatro.

It was customary for vessels to do this when they were off duty. The GPS came back at 3.10 AM and then headed to the airport, and after a drop off at Lido, the boat moored outside Luca's house all night. The next day it was picked up by the club staff and brought back to the clubhouse, where it remained moored until Mia took it out three days later.

Anna told Senn that the police had already issued search warrants for all the tourists Luca had picked up. She was waiting for a copy of the list to discuss with him how to proceed. The other thing they were still searching for was Luca's missing phone from the flat.

Senn was nervous about the planned detour he wanted to make to Luca's flat to satisfy his obsessive hunch without keeping Anna in the loop.

Senn considered Anna the surrogate Venetian police. Thanks to her influence inside the police HQ, they could access privileged information about the case.

But this time, he was breaching the trust code and challenging the police's prognosis. He felt it would be easier for Anna not to agree to do something she would find hard to explain to the cops later.

Senn pulled his jacket hood tightly over his head and stepped gingerly into the face-numbing windy night. He briskly walked through the narrow, scantily lit Calle del Tragheto, and jumped into the waiting taxi boat heading to Luca's flat in St. Elena.

Senn knew he was taking a considerable risk by reponing the Luca can of worms, but he felt there was still some evidence in the flat that could pinpoint Laura's location. An address, a telephone number, something he might have written down that was still in the flat but unknown to the people who hired him for the mission and later killed him to shut him up.

Arriving at the flat, he noticed Luca's neighbor's light was still on. Careful not to attract attention, Senn crept to the back of the flat, climbed under the police tape, and turned the handle of the metal service door. Senn was sure it would be open because it was a joint service door to the building and used by the people who lived a floor above him.

He tiptoed up to the flat door and studied the locked door for a few seconds under torchlight. Then, from his jacket zipper, Senn removed a thin, pencil-length metal rod with a small hook at its end, inserted it into the keyhole, and gently turned his way through the tumblers inside the lock until it clicked open. Senn smirked. He'd learned his lock picking from Ali, the fastest locksmith in Amsterdam (also reverently called Alibaba in the lock-picking circles).

The cold, pitch-dark, congested space still carried a stale smell of cigarettes, and the food was possibly starting to rot inside the fridge, adding to the foul odor in the room. Senn entered and began his search through a small rack of papers on his kitchen table.

A thick stack of used lottery stubs lay in a pile next to a bunch of gasoline receipts. A few calling cards for nightclubs and phone sex chat cards were in the same bundle. Senn moved next to his bed and rummaged through some newspapers, all folded on the crossword page, with most of them complete. Senn gave a slight grin, admiring Luca's secret intellectual skills.

Like the rest of the orderly flat, Senn opened the wardrobe to find the clothes, t-shirts, jeans, and shirts neatly piled on each other. Above them, about six white captain uniforms hung in a row. He looked around for a few seconds and was about to close the door when he spotted a little red diary sticking out of one of the pockets of the uniforms.

Senn opened it, and his eyes narrowed. It showed dates, time slots, telephone numbers, and addresses scrawled across pages. He moved down the list until he came to the last entry, which made his hair stand on end.

It read,

Una Borsa, Dario, 4th February, Lido.

CHAPTER 18

THE BAG IN LIDO

"To save all, we must risk all."

—FRIEDRICH VON SCHILLER

Senn felt energized as he tucked Luca's planner into his jacket. He was sure he'd found a vital clue to Laura's location.

The last planner entry resounded in his mind as he tiptoed out of the flat.

Una Borsa, Dario, 4th February, Lido.

The cryptic reference to *a bag* and the date, 4th Feb, coincided with the date Laura went missing. Dario could be someone Luca had done business with before. Senn made a mental note to tally this name with the police. When he returned to his room, he needed to check the planner in more detail. But the cursory glance at the pages confirmed his hunch that Luca was part of the Venetian mafia and did routine pick-ups and drops for them, and Laura could have been his last assignment before his death.

Senn strode briskly as the icy wind from the inky black canal waters buffeted his face. The sidewalks lay deserted as the church tower struck 4 AM. He found his way to an electric scooter stand in a cul de sac and unlocked one of the scooters in the parking lot for his ride home.

Just as his bike sputtered to life, Senn heard a dog's startled bark from the street right behind him that turned into incessant barking. A light came on above the bike stand, someone opened a window, and a furry black cat slid out. It froze and stared at Senn first and then at something behind him with piercing, scared eyes. Senn turned his head to spot a silhouette slink out of view from the corner of his eye.

Senn tensed as his eyes darted nervously into the darkness. After the last attack, Senn had become hyper-vigilant about suspicious movements around him. Senn's heart raced as he pulled away and headed back to his flat. Someone was tailing him.

Senn zipped through the deserted streets of Venice with filigreed streetlights casting haunting shadows on the crumbling walls while his mind battled the dangers that seemed to shadow him constantly. Senn kept checking his rear-view mirrors for any signs of being followed but saw nothing.

He reached his apartment and was about to put his key into the main door when he saw something that made him freeze. At the end of the dimly lit road was an outline of a man seated on a bike smoking a cigarette, his face hidden under a hooded jacket, looking straight in his direction. The man started at Senn for a few seconds, drew the last puff of the cigarette, then flicked the burning butt into the canal and started his bike.

Senn shouted, "Hey, you. Stop," and started sprinting toward him to try and catch the man or at least get a glimpse of his face. Seeing Senn coming at him, the biker put his head down, revved his bike, sped down the road, and quickly disappeared into the long, dark alleyways.

Senn ran up to where the man was and looked down to see two cigarillo butts on the floor. Senn carefully collected the butts and carried them back to his apartment to save as evidence he wanted to analyze further.

The man's spunk rattled Senn. He seemed unfrazzled and fearless in the way he taunted Senn from a safe distance. Maybe it was time for Senn to ask for some police escort in the city. He felt the mafia was getting bolder and maybe turning bitter because he was not backing off his search.

The following day, Senn was the first to arrive at the police HQ.

Colonel Taino had called the meeting and asked him and Anna to attend and brief him on the progress. Anna arrived a few minutes late, looking a bit ragged and beady-eyed.

"Hey," she said as she slumped in the chair next to him.

"Hey," replied Senn with a slight smirk. "Too early?"

Anna shook her head as she rubbed her eyes and replied, "Party."

The colonel's secretary walked up and escorted them to his office, where the colonel sat peering into a miniature ship encased inside a bottle.

He gave Anna a tight bear hug and then vigorously shook Senn's hand. Then he said, "'The Impossible Bottle' was first made in Venice at the start of the 18th century, and I have just found one of the last ones made here." He jubilantly picked up the aged, thick glass bottle with an intricately carved naval sail ship inside, still looking as fresh as its first day of mast hoisting.

Grinning like a kid in a candy store, the colonel admired the bottled ship for a few more seconds and then carefully placed it at the head of his enormous mahogany table.

Then he looked at Senn and Anna and said, "I hear you've found the boat and the captain. Let me restate, *the dead* captain?"

Senn and Anna nodded and looked on as the colonel pulled out something from his drawers while talking.

In the colonel's hands was a tightly packed plastic packet containing a white, cake-like substance that he handed Anna to examine.

"The same boat also had 100 kgs of this stashed in its hull."

Senn looked at the packet and instantly recognized it was cocaine.

Looking surprised, Anna kept quiet and waited for the colonel to explain.

The colonel nodded at Senn as he confirmed it was indeed cocaine, and police sniffer dogs had discovered it hidden inside a secret compartment under the hull. He reluctantly commented that Mia and Stephan had immediately claimed no knowledge of this.

"But we have taken them into custody anyway, and they are with their lawyers right now sorting out bail." The colonel shrugged as he put the cocaine packet back into his drawer.

Senn squinted at Anna as a new motive sprang up in his mind.

Mother and son kidnapped Laura because she'd somehow found the drugs while on the boat and wanted to report it to the police.

CHAPTER 19

THE LINKED CUFFS OF MIA, STEPHAN, AND LUCA

Colonel Taino's furrowed brow and piercing blue eyes burrowed into the red diary Senn had found in Luca's house, while the safety deposit box key Senn had found in Laura's bag sat in the middle of his desk.

He scanned the pages as his eyes darted from Senn back to the diary. Anna sat quietly as both men battled their wits about the possible motives for staging Luca's assassination. Senn laid out his rationale while Taino paced around the office, diary still in hand.

"But, Senn, why would someone kill Luca and make the effort of staging it? If it were the mafia, they would kill him and leave," Taino asked while rubbing his neck with his muscular hands.

Senn had asked himself the same question. The only answer he could muster was that Luca's killer wanted to remove all evidence of Laura's abduction.

Senn believed Luca was hand-picked as the ideal sacrificial lamb. He was a reclusive man known to the police for his petty crime, drinking problems, and suicidal tendencies. He had tried to commit suicide by slashing his wrists once in prison but was unsuccessful. What Senn found more intriguing was that Luca's killers had profiled him well before making him the courier of the operation.

Senn voiced his theory to Taino, who pensively nodded as he flicked through the diary again. He walked to his desk, read something from the stack of papers on his table, and said, "Mia confessed she and Stephan knew Luca well. He used to visit them at their beach house in Malamocco. He would drive them there and stay over for the weekend."

Senn found that rather odd.

The fact that Stephan and Mia would entertain a relatively well-known Venetian mafia operative at their beach house suggested they might have deeper links to the mafia than he had first imagined.

But it made something else weaker. It reduced the chances that Mia and Stephan would intentionally harm Luca *unless* they were grooming him and intended to dispose of him if he got too close.

Senn was beginning to see a faint pattern that he laid out in front of Anna and the colonel.

Senn hypothesized Laura had somehow uncovered Stephan and Mia's drug racketeering inside the Teatro and threatened to either leave or go to the police. To secure her safety, Laura stole Stephan's safety deposit key before confronting them.

To silence her, Stephan and Mia contacted Luca, a friend and maybe a business associate in drug trafficking, who managed to lure Laura onto their boat. Then he somehow knocked her unconscious, ferried her under the boats' seats, and deposited her somewhere with the help of Dario, an accomplice.

But then Mia and Stephan somehow got suspicious of Luca.

Either of his loose tongue or maybe he started blackmailing them. Then, the mother and son hired an assassin to eliminate Luca and make it seem like an unrelated, self-inflicted death.

They chose someone (Dario?) who Luca knew and trusted enough to let into his house (as there was no forced entry on the night of his death).

But this evidence meant Mia and Stephan plotted the operation, hired an assassin to neutralize Luca, and knew where Laura was.

Senn was sure Laura was still alive as Mia and Stephan were not sure who else she had tattled her drug finding to and was refusing to tell them where the security deposit box key was. Therefore, they were still interrogating her somewhere.

Anna listened intently to Senn through his rendition and then raised her hand, asking permission to interject.

Senn paused, curious about what her assessment would be.

"But if Mia and Stephan tried to hide that they are peddling drugs, why did they leave the cocaine in the boat? They should have removed it."

The colonel interjected, "I also find it strange that the boat was carrying 100 kgs of cocaine, and they left it untouched. Mia called us and you both at around the same time with the discovery of Laura's wallet. She had enough time to dispose of the drugs before calling us."

Anna chipped in excitedly, "But to play devil's advocate, they left the drugs in the boat to prove their innocence of the crime. They wanted us to know that they knew nothing about all the crime!"

Despite many doubts, Senn sensed that Anna and the colonel were starting to believe his theory.

At that moment, an officer knocked and entered, walked up to the colonel, and whispered something into his ear.

The colonel listened with lowered eyes covered by the thick bushel of his shaggy eyebrows. He nodded and said, "Thanks, Mikkey. Take them both there right now."

The colonel looked grim as he tapped his desk and said, "They just found the dead body of a man in Lido. He had a bullet in his head, and someone had plastered the words *Porco* across his chest with his blood. The mafia does this to shame someone for being a traitor."

After another pause, he looked at Senn and said, "His name was Dario."

CHAPTER 20

COMBING THE SANDS OF LIDO

"One must be cold if one wishes to savor chaos."

—FERDINAND HARDEKOPF

Senn could feel Anna's nervousness as they approached the draped corpse of Dario at the Lido police station morgue.

The doctor pulled the cover to reveal a surprisingly boyish face with curly blonde hair lying naked on a sparkling stainless-steel stretcher. He had crusty sand in his long hair and nose, and crusted lumps of blood mixed with sand covering the back of his head and neck where the bullet had punctured his skull. There were no other marks of struggle on the rest of his athletically built, pale torso. The word *Porco* was scribbled across his chest with his blood in a rather meticulous and striking fashion. Almost like a painter signing their artwork.

Senn leaned forward and looked closely at the bloodied scrawl across his chest, instantly noticing the coincidence. He took out his phone and flicked back to the photographs of the mirror in Luca's bathroom, where he supposedly scrawled his two-word suicide note. He turned the phone to Anna as he whispered to her, "The *P*. Look at the letter *P*." Anna turned and leaned forward to inspect.

The *P* was inscribed with the same loopy swirl on the curve as on the *P* in the words *Perdonami Padre* found in Luca's bathroom.

The same!

Anna looked at the close resemblance in the writing style, looked at Senn, and nodded. Senn could see that Anna was starting to agree with Senn that Luca was murdered and could also be Dario's assassin.

The beady-eyed, bespeckled coroner lady informed them that Dario had died in the early morning hours with a single shot at close range to the back of his head. No struggle marks on the body or any sign of heightened adrenaline in his blood. It seemed Dario died at the hands of someone he knew and trusted. Again, very similar to how Luca had treated his eventual assassins.

Someone had betrayed Luca and Dario.

Senn inquired about the location of the body. The police captain showed them pictures of Dario lying face down on a remote edge of the Lido beach. The killers had taken their time to clean the area around the body as they had done in Luca's apartment. The captain added that they were still carrying out fingerprint and DNA tests and did not know any more details.

The only ID proof they had found in the car or the victim's body was Dario's gym membership card that had fallen under his seat, which the assassins had been unable to find. But apart from this, he was squeaky clean.

Captain Mikkey rode in the front as Anna and Senn sat in the back seat heading to Dario's apartment.

Anna was unusually quiet and tense throughout their journey to Dario's place.

Senn felt he was partly to blame.

Earlier in the morning, she was visibly upset when Senn showed her Luca's diary and confessed to making a second solo visit to the crime scene. She was angry that he had not trusted her with his plans. Senn tried to justify his actions to protect Anna, but it had little or no impact on her mood and demeanor.

Senn was now worried he may have created a trust gap between them. That bothered him. Over the past few days, he had grown to value Anna's proactiveness and astute intelligence. Senn made a mental note to level with her after they finished checking out Dario's flat.

On the way to the flat, the captain gave them a quick download of what they knew about Dario.

Dario was 22 and single. He worked in the Lido gym as an instructor, doubled as the front office manager, and just started driving water taxis as a side hustle. Senn found it interesting as he scanned his file that Dario had received his Vaporetto driver's license just a week ago. That would make his trip with Luca one of his first. Senn wondered if his assassin knew that and planned the kidnapping accordingly.

The captain continued talking fast, explaining how Dario had recently moved into his flat about six months ago from Perugia after completing a college degree in tourism. He did not have any previous criminal records.

So Dario, unlike Luca, was clean and a newbie at the crime scene. Senn wondered how much Dario knew about the operation. Or was he just a driver? Also, Senn was confused about why the assassin had booked two Vaporetto drivers for the job.

The flat was on the fourth floor in a modern high-rise multiplex. They entered to see local police officers rummaging through his belongings. After introductions, Anna asked the officers for a quick briefing.

Senn immediately felt something stir in the room.

He was having a soul flash.

Senn saw Dario staring at Senn as he sat on the open windowsill with his legs dangling outside. He was wearing a black polo neck jumper and blue jeans and reading a book, the cover of which Senn could not make out. He glanced at Senn briefly, gave him a rueful smile, and, without warning, jumped off the ledge.

Senn reacted instinctively and dashed to the window to see what lay below. It was the parking lot of the building lined with cars and jeeps.

Anna jumped a bit, startled at Senn's sudden movements. She looked at him with a smirk and asked, "What? Another ghost."

Senn apologized and pried his eyes away from Anna's inquisitive stare.

He sat to catch his breath and recover from the soul flash.

CHAPTER 21

LIDO UNLOCKS THE WAY

Senn stared at the spot they had found Dario's body in the sand while the wind wrestled with the angry waves in the distance.

The ocean had swept away all the evidence on the crime scene. It was a lonely spot with no houses or hotels except a decrepit lighthouse in the far east. Lido was a hot beach spot for the rich and famous, but that was a few miles north.

Anna walked beside the brooding Senn, looked out at the empty beach, and said, "Dario knew Laura's location. Maybe that's why they killed him."

Senn nodded. "Most likely. His name's in Luca's diary, and the boat was here that night."

Senn's analysis of the GPS data showed the boat had docked close to the Teatro at 1 AM on the morning of the 4th of February, and then the GPS signal had been switched off for two hours. The boat then made one last trip to Lido, returned to Luca's house, and parked there for the rest of the night.

Lido was the boat's last stop that night. But where and how did the captors move Laura?

Before Senn could ask, the captain got a call informing him to return to Dario's place. They had found Dario's gym van in his parking lot with over 100 kgs of cocaine stashed inside!

Senn's eyes lit up with hope. If they were using the van to transport drugs from and to the island, the van must have clues to finding Laura.

They rushed back to Dario's apartment block and saw the police cordoning it off, and sniffer dogs were in the van. The residents had popped their heads out of the windows and peaked at the goings below. The news of Dario's death and the cocaine in his car spread fast. As they passed through the crowded parking lot, an older woman talked excitedly, telling an officer how she knew Dario as a lovely, kind boy who helped her with her groceries once in a while. She looked sad and confused.

Senn and Anna made their way to meet the police officer leading the investigation. The officer led them to a temporary enclosure to show them the van's contents.

The cocaine packets were tightly taped together and wrapped in black bin bags. Senn picked up a bag and could tell the packages were from the same consignment found in the boat. Next to the bags lay all the things found in the van.

A Roma football club banner lay tangled among empty cigarette packets, crumpled McDonald's paper bags, pizza boxes, and a paperback copy of *The Power of Positive Thinking* by Norman Vincent Peale. Underlined in many places, and some chapters had been dog-eared. Anna glanced at the book and raised her eyebrows. "A nerdy drug dealer. Rare."

Next to the laden keychain, Senn spotted receipts sticking out from one of the empty fast food paper bags.

They were supermarket receipts. Senn's brows furrowed as he went down the list. Besides numerous food items, the shopping list contained sizeable spending on clothes, heating equipment, and water. He noticed the receipts' address was from a Supermercato in Via Lungo Adige. Senn googled the address and found it was on the island's south side. He turned to the captain and asked, "Is this close to Dario's gym?"

The captain looked at the address and remarked, "No, it's close to Alberoni, on the south side."

Senn looked at the keys attached to the chain. "What are these extra keys, captain?"

The captain replied, "Not sure, but the owner mentioned that they have a warehouse in Alberoni where they store old equipment, but he rarely uses it. Maybe they belong to the warehouse."

Senn exclaimed, "Why are we waiting? Let's go."

Senn's hopes spurred as he and Anna jumped into the police van and headed to the warehouse. Senn could sense they were close to Laura.

The journey from Lido beach to Alberoni was down a pencil-thin, partly metalled and part gravel ocean road on the island's south side. The further south they traveled, the sparser it got with raw graffiti on walls and abandoned cars and boats crowded together in open brownfields. It was nearing sunset, and the wind was picking up the cold draft from the ocean and slamming it into the giant Cyprus trees along the roadside.

They arrived at the gym's warehouse's small, weather-beaten, rusted shutter. It was an unmarked building with paint peeling off the walls and damp marks of rising humidity from the floor. Senn and Anna waited patiently as the police captain struggled with the lock on the shutter. Eventually, one of the keys fitted, and the metal sheet rolled open with a menacing grating sound. Senn prepared himself for the worst as he followed the captain's high-powered torch into the eerie darkness.

The cavernous, dank room was stone-cold empty.

Senn bent and touched the floor with his fingers. It was sparkling clean. Someone had removed whatever was inside and bleached it.

Senn turned to Anna and the captain and said with a shrug, "They knew we were coming."

Anna spotted something and walked past Senn towards a door at the far corner of the room. She pulled her jumper sleeve over her fingers and turned the handle. It was the toilet.

Switching the lights, they could see empty blank interiors, including the scrubbed plastic cupboard over the small, chipped sink.

Senn stood looking at his reflection in the cracked, frameless mirror, trying to hide his disappointment. He silently prayed Laura had not been tortured or mistreated inside these four grim walls.

The level of cleaning was reminiscent of Luca's house. It's as if the perpetrators wanted to rub out all signs of activity inside.

Senn was worried for Laura's life now.

He kept staring, trying to imagine the faces that had looked in the same mirror.

In the reflection, his eyes caught something on the wall next to the toilet seat.

Scratched on the wall were four chilling letters.

H E L P

CHAPTER 22

TANTALISING DEAD ENDS

"Good judgment is the result of experience and experience the result of bad judgment."

—MARK TWAIN

Anna examined the crudely scratched *Help* graffiti on the wall as Senn searched the warehouse for any other signs of Laura's presence.

The stark, chipped, red-brick walls had a few torn and faded posters of rippling bodybuilders posing in one corner and some large, empty boxes stacked at another end of the room. The 5-meter-high ceiling had a retractable skylight that was beginning to catch a few heavy raindrops.

Anna confirmed that the scratches were recent and made with a sharp, metal object or a bottle cap based on some silver paint still embedded in the grooves of the words. But she'd found nothing else.

The captain added that he had called the forensic team to check for fingerprints, and they would come tomorrow. He also confirmed that the interrogation of the gym owner had not borne any clues. The 60-year-old retired schoolteacher had recently opened the gym and denied any knowledge of the drug smuggling or Dario's wrongdoings from his warehouse. The owner had even agreed to take a polygraph test to prove his innocence.

The captain reckoned the man could be telling the truth. It was typical for the mafia sometimes to use the premises of unsuspecting ordinary people to carry out their nefarious operations.

Senn stood perplexed and frustrated, cracking his knuckles in the middle of the echoing warehouse, feeling tantalizingly close to Laura yet out of reach.

They'd hit a dead end again.

She was most likely brought to this place on the 4th and kept here for some days. Based on Dario's shopping receipts that stopped on the 7th of February, Dario was found dead on the 9th, a day after Luca's death. Senn surmised Laura must have been in the warehouse until at least the 8th of February, which was a week ago.

Anna looked at her watch, glanced at Senn, and said, "Are we done, Senn? We can come back if we think of something else. Right, captain?" The captain nodded as he pulled down the shutter and assured them he would assist with future requests and keep them updated on the findings.

Senn reluctantly walked out into the howling wind from the ocean in the distance. As Anna turned the ignition, she remarked, looking worried, "We better get back. There's a storm coming."

Senn's mind clawed with alternative explanations while the wipers in Anna's Jeep struggled to mop away the unrelenting downpour on the drive back to the Lido jetty.

Unlike Senn, Anna was in an upbeat, talkative mood.

"It reminds me of Luca's place for another reason. It smells the same. Whoever cleaned Luca's place cleaned this place. Or could it be a coincidence?" Anna asked, looking curiously at Senn.

After a few seconds of contemplation, he nodded. "Luca's killers probably planned to kill Dario, too, so they could have bought enough detergent and cleaning equipment to clear both places."

Senn voiced his real worry, "But what I don't get is if they are such cold-blooded psychopaths, why have they kept Laura alive for so long? They must be looking for the key. But I still can't figure out how she got hold of it in the first place."

Anna cautiously replied, "We don't know if Laura's *still* alive. She could be dead, and we just haven't found her yet."

Senn nodded but looked away. He was not ready to go there.

Not yet. Hopefully never.

He still harbored a nagging doubt that there was something he had overlooked back at the warehouse but was worried that neither Anna nor the police captain would agree to go back and recheck his hunch in this downpour.

Feeling restless, Senn flicked through the pictures he'd taken at the warehouse to see if something stood out. As he poured over the images, something caught his eye. It was an unremarkable picture of the empty warehouse that Senn had taken to record the place's cleanliness.

But he noticed something odd on the floor.

The tungsten light had magnified the heavily scratched floor tiles except for a faint one square meter outline on the floor amid the scratches. Senn stared at the picture and blew it up in magnification to look at the details. He turned to Anna and asked, "Can you see this tile on the floor? It's an odd shape in the middle of the room, and no other tile is cut to the same size. What do you think?"

Anna looked at the picture and shrugged, unimpressed. "They must have kept something on that area that stained the section. It's a warehouse. Some parts get used more than others."

Senn shook his head, stared steadfastly at Anna, and in a monotone replied, "Could be, but I want to check it out again. I'm sorry to do this, but we must go back."

Anna rolled her eyes in disbelief, looking incredulously at Senn. "Right now!? We're in the middle of a storm and might miss the last boat back. Can't we come back tomorrow?"

But Senn was defiant. If Laura was still alive, she was somewhere on this island, but time was running out. Whoever was moving her around could get nervous and make rash decisions. Senn had to follow his instinct and reinvestigate the warehouse. He offered to call the captain, ask for permission, and explain his hunch.

Reluctantly, Anna gave Senn the phone to talk to the captain ahead of them in the traffic. Unconvinced, but on Senn's insistence, the captain agreed to hand over the keys and let them check the place out again.

Senn could see Anna was angry at Senn's stubbornness. She grumbled and complained about the worsening weather as they turned around and headed back to the warehouse. When they reached the place again, it was desolate, choked up with ankle-deep water, and pitch dark.

While Anna waited, Senn offered to go and check the place, but she refused. So, after a few minutes of struggling with the lock, the soaking-wet Senn and Anna re-entered the warehouse.

Senn found the electric mains and turned the lights on, then zeroed in on the spot on the floor at the far corner of the room. It was a small, one-square-meter section with no grooves or holes in it. Senn bent and looked for edges or grooves to pry open the tile but found none. He pressed down the tile in various sections, but nothing happened either.

Unflapped, Senn got up and walked back to the electricity meter board at the entrance, scanned the switches in the box, and noticed that all the cut-outs were on except one. He'd noticed this anomaly when looking for the electricity mains earlier. The moment he turned the switch, they heard a clicking sound, and to their amazement, the tile on the floor lifted an inch out of the ground.

Senn's eyes lit up. What was under that door?

CHAPTER 23

WHEN A DOOR CLOSES, A TRAP OPENS

Anna looked on as Senn climbed down through the narrow shaft of the trap door hatch into the vacuous basement.

Excited by the discovery, Senn wanted to enter and explore immediately, but Anna dug her heels and refused to go down. "I feel claustrophobic," Anna said in an anxious, pleading voice.

Senn nodded and replied, "Wait for me. I'll check it out."

Anna nodded, looking relieved.

Senn descended the narrow, damp steps, flashlight in hand. As his eyes adjusted to the light, he noticed that it wasn't a room but a thin, wet passage headed west. After walking about fifty steps, the path reached a locked metal door. Senn put his ear to the door and heard the sound of crashing waves from the other side, and the air had that distinct smell of rotting fish.

He inspected the lock. It was a cheap padlock that Senn picked after a few minutes of tinkering. The latch made a loud squeaking noise that echoed in the passage as Senn pushed the door open and shined his light at what lay on the other side.

He was stunned at what he saw.

The door opened into a large, hollow, hooded stone cave with long, dangling vines obscuring the view out to the sea, and barnacles and thick moss growing all over its old, veinous rock face. About five or six artificial stone steps led to the foot of the cave, which lay submerged under seawater. Senn reckoned it was low tide, but the whole place could fill and flood the passage he'd just walked down during high tide.

Senn smirked at how perfect this spot was for smugglers to come and go as long as they timed their entry. He shined his light on the walls and noticed three large mooring bolts screwed into the stone at regular intervals.

Senn had uncovered a secret docking point, probably owned by the mafia.

He imagined three to four boats regularly loading and offloading goods here and then the warehouse serving as a storage and distribution point for further delivery.

Senn could see that this was not a one-person operation, but a well-planned and sophisticated process continuously run by a much bigger group.

Senn was sure that if Laura were in the warehouse, she would have traveled through this passage and cave.

He peered through the gaping hole of the dark cave into the angry, stormy ocean and silently prayed for Laura's safety. Senn felt tortured by the feeling she was close and yet obscured by some invisible wall.

Senn walked back and climbed up the shaft until his head re-emerged into the warehouse to see Anna pacing the floor, looking pale and restless.

Senn pulled himself out of the trap door and looked at Anna inquiringly. "Is everything ok?"

Anna, looking grim, replied, "Nothing. This place is spooky. What did you find?" Senn told her, and her eyes widened in disbelief. And then, in a halting voice, she said, "I know that cave. We used to go there when we were kids. But I never knew it had a secret passage to this place! I can show you. Come."

Anna and Senn walked out, waded through ankle-deep water, and jumped into her car. Senn noticed Anna was wearing black combat boots, which were soaking wet as they made squishing sounds when she stepped into the Jeep. Senn tried to empathize with her shoes and said, "Sorry about your shoes."

Surprised by the comment, Anna looked down at her shoes, giggled, and replied, "Yes, I love my boots, and I bought these last week. But it looks like I'll need new ones soon."

Senn laughed back, looked at his biker boots, and sighed. "Me too!"

They laughed and released some of the pent-up tension between them. They were both high-strung, and a few sparks were natural.

Anna turned the Jeep left and headed towards the island's southern edge. The rain and wind had mellowed, and the clouds were beginning to shift, revealing a clear sky and an almost full moon just rising in the sky.

After about a kilometer, she reached the end of the road. The streetlights in this area were a bit better, with a single lamp flickering erratically.

Anna parked and walked down a steep dirt road that descended towards the ocean below. After walking about twenty steps, the path abruptly ended with a long stone ledge sticking out above the sea about thirty feet high. With a glint in her eyes, Anna turned to Senn. "If you want to see the cave, you have to walk to the edge, lie on the stone, and look under the wall. The cave is right there. Or you can jump into the ocean and swim into it."

Senn looked amused. "How do you know all this?"

Anna laughed. "The cave was our hideout from our parents. This door is new, so the mafia discovered it after we did."

Senn was a little taken aback that Anna knew this remote location so well. Surprised, he asked, "How often did you come here?"

Anna shrugged with a sheepish grin and said, "Oh, not that often. Once or twice, I think. I had forgotten all about it."

Senn nodded as he anxiously stared into the inky darkness of the Venetian lagoon and wondered where the boats went from the cave and which one ferried Laura.

CHAPTER 24

MIA WANTS TO TALK

"Hope is a waking dream."

—ARISTOTLE

Senn hung up the phone. Mia had urgently asked to meet him for lunch. He grimaced at his reflection in the mirror. Dark circles, his bushy beard, and curling hair ends behind his ears added years to his otherwise lean torso.

He thought she sounded a little scared as he finished his daily 100 push-ups, 100 crunches calisthenic workout, and poured himself a cup of tea while breathing in the crisp air and bright sunrise over the Grand Canal.

Mia had just bailed herself and Stephan out of prison a day ago after spending a night in jail on charges of drug trafficking. The news of Mia and Stephan in prison had spread like wildfire in the city.

The local daily had published a cover story showing the facade of the Teatro Rossi and her boat moored outside the police station claiming that Mia and Stephan were involved in running a drug cartel from the theatre.

The article speculated that the theatre was just a front for the drug cartel that Stephan ran with his mother to pay for the renovation and repairs of the theatre, devastated by a fire two years ago. A theory Senn found compelling.

He combed through the details but was surprised to see the article only mentioned the mother and son concerning the drugs and did not mention the disappearance of Laura or the death of Luca and Dario.

Senn had a lot of questions for Mia since his return from Lido late last night. He wanted to ask her about Luca, Dario, the warehouse, and the hidden underground passage to the ocean cave. The duo had confessed that they knew Luca as a friend who had visited them a few times at their beach house on Lido but had reiterated that they knew nothing about his links to the Mafia or the drug cartels.

By the time Senn reached Mia's designated canal-side restaurant, it was almost 1 PM.

Mia sat on the far corner sofa with her back to the gilded oval mirror on the wall, looking out to the busy canal on her right. Her powder-soft, fluffy, white hair snugly cupped her delicate, oval face but contrasted sharply with her anxious, darting eyes and flaming red lipstick.

Mia sighed with relief when Senn walked up, shook her hand, and sat. Senn could sense Mia was in a dithery state. Her white wine glass was almost empty, and her bag's contents lay strewn on the seat next to her.

Mia covered her face with the table napkin and whispered, "Mr. Senn, I think someone's following me."

Senn's smiling face crumpled into a frown as he leaned forward and replied in a concerned voice, "Is the person here right now?"

Mia shook her head and, with a slight tremble, said, "No, but he was following me until I entered this place. He knows I am here." Senn scanned the crowd of tourists and well-heeled Venetians busy in animated conversation within their groups as tuxedoed servers scurried around delivering and taking orders in this upscale trattoria at the corner of Palazzo Franchetti.

"What did he look like?" Senn asked, trying to calm her.

"He was a horrible, rude, tall, lanky man," Mia replied, her eyes still darting nervously at the canal boats as she took a big gulp and emptied her wine glass. "I knew he was following me because he kept smiling at me with this strange, crazed look in his eyes."

Mia paused and continued, "I've never seen him before. He's got this lean, bony face with hollow cheeks and dark, hooded eyes, and his teeth have this ugly brown stain across them. He's scary, Mr. Senn!"

Senn was shocked at her description.

Mia was describing the *same man* who had mugged him in the alleyway! Senn had not caught all his features as clearly during the attack, but the stained teeth on a tall, bony frame were a sure match.

Senn tried to squelch his excitement as he leaned forward and asked, "Do you remember anything else about him?"

"Yes," Mia exclaimed. "He was wearing these brown embroidered cowboy leather boots. I noticed them, especially because when I first spotted him, he sat sideways on a motorbike outside my house, smoking a cigarette when I exited. He blankly stared at me and then started grinning like a madman. It felt creepy as hell, Mr. Senn!"

Senn was almost sure they were talking about the same man Senn had seen outside his flat the night he'd come back from Luca's house. Even though he had not caught the man's face, Senn had caught the unusually designed boots in the streetlight as he sped away.

Mia, who he considered a suspect, was being followed and bullied by the same man who assaulted and tailed him.

Strange. Senn had not expected this twist in the quest.

If Mia were guilty, she would not face threats by the same man who threatened him to stay away from the investigation and the Teatro. Senn remembered the black-winged tattoo on the man's palm, marking him as a Venetian mafia member. So if Mia were in cahoots with the mafia, she would not be harassed by the mafia.

Or were they keeping her in line?

Senn began to question for the first time if someone was framing Mia for the drugs and (even Laura's disappearance).

While still making sense of the new information, Senn leaned back and asked, "Why do you think he's harassing you?"

Before Mia could answer, a young teenage boy burst into the restaurant and stood in front of Mia and Senn. Still out of breath, he handed Mia a folded paper bag and said, "He said happy birthday."

The boy dropped the packet and bolted before they could react, disappearing around the corner.

Senn tried to give chase, but the kid was too quick. Senn returned to the table to see Mia in tears. She looked in total disarray as her hands trembled at what she held. Senn slowly looked down to see what it was.

It was an old color photograph of a smiling young woman holding a wrapped newborn in her arms. Senn instantly recognized who it was.

It was Mia's adolescent face.

CHAPTER 25

MIA'S SECRET

"Don't wait to be hunted to hide."

—SAMUEL BECKETT

Senn felt compassion for Mia as she silently wept while hugging the faded picture of her radiant adolescent self, cradling a newborn.

Mia, usually the impregnable charismatic woman, was crumbling under the pressure of being brazenly stalked and then rudely fronted with a photograph of her veiled past. On top of her pending drug trafficking charges and a night in jail, this bizarre encounter only added fuel to Mia's frazzled state.

But that didn't preclude Senn's curiosity about the picture and the cryptic message parroted with it. Who was the newborn in the photo?

Mia spoke in a quivering voice as she placed the photograph on the table for Senn to get a good look at for the first time. "This is my daughter. She lived for three days."

Shocked by the confession, Senn replied, "I'm so sorry, Mia. What happened to her?"

Looking sad and withdrawn, Mia replied in a strained voice, "The doctors said she got meningitis and died in her sleep."

Senn looked at the photo again, this time with heightened empathy. He could tell Mia was shaken by the revelation but relieved by her confession.

"Who else knew about her?" Senn inquired, trying to explain her link with the stalker.

"Nobody," came her abrupt, stony reply.

Mia quickly recovered her poise but looked worried. Then in a scared tone, she said, "You need to find this man, Mr. Senn. He is trying to hurt me. I'll pay you whatever you want."

Surprised by her sudden change of tone and blank cheque offer, Senn replied cautiously, "I can't help you until you tell me everything you know."

Mia momentarily glared at Senn before lowering her gaze back to the photograph. "OK, what do you want to know?"

Senn, for the first time, felt Mia was ready to talk. Something inside her had snapped.

Senn steadied his gaze and cleared his throat. "Mia, I need to find Laura. Her life is in danger. What can you tell me that might help me?"

Mia knitted her brow. "Laura saw something in the Teatro that she wanted to show Stephan."

"What did she see?" Senn asked bluntly

"I'm not sure, but I think it was the drugs."

"Why would she spot drugs in the Teatro? You told the police you knew nothing about it."

In a halting voice, Mia paused and said, "Yes, that's true, but I think someone put the drugs in the basement."

Senn sighed with frustration. "Mia, stop playing around with me. No more games, please."

Mia, now visibly frightened, "Mr. Senn, the Teatro is owned by the mafia."

Alarm bells rang out in Senn's head when he heard these words.

"I thought you and Stephan were the owners," Senn said calmly as his mind raced, joining the dots.

Mia shook her head as tears rolled down her cheeks. "On paper. They practically control everything."

So Mia was fronting a mafia operation with her celebrity son in the middle of the arty Venice theatre district!

"So what all do you cover up for them?" Senn asked, still reeling from the confession.

"We look the other way." She continued tiredly, "We don't interfere in their business, and they let us do ours. They operate out of the basement. It's their space, and we don't ask them questions. And Laura somehow went down there and saw something and wanted to show it to Stephan the night she went missing. That is all I know. I swear on my son's life."

Still unsatisfied with the answer, Senn interjected, "But why are you telling me all this? Aren't you scared the mafia will come after you?

Mia nervously sipped her second glass of wine. "Yes, I'm scared. I think they've decided to hurt Stephan and me. They think we ratted on them. That's why I asked to see you today. I need your help."

CHAPTER 26

MIA'S MAFIA CONNECTION

"My past is everything I failed to be."

—FERNANDO PESSOA

Mia sank back into her seat and hid her trembling hands under the table to calm her nerves as the servers brought the steaming hot lunch.

Senn could see she was distracted and scared as she nervously glanced at the food and tried to converse politely with the servers who knew her well.

Senn still had a lot of unanswered questions for Mia.

He waited for the staff to leave and then leaned forward and inquired, "Do you know these people who *use* your theatre?"

Mia's eyes narrowed as she tried to recall some things, and then she said, "No, I've never met any of them. They only communicate via hand-delivered notes. I think Stephan's met some of them."

"Why did you let the mafia use your basement?" Senn asked curiously.

Mia sighed deeply. "It was after the fire."

Senn kept quiet but raised his eyebrows and waited for Mia to explain.

Mia talked between bites of her Penne Arrabiata and said, "Mr. Senn, two years ago, the Teatro was an architectural marvel and attracted some of the best artists and shows in Venice. Stephan was also getting a lot of critical acclaim for his quality of direction and scale of productions. We were happy."

Mia's pride and love for the Teatro were evident in her voice and gestures to Senn.

But tears welled up again as she stuttered, "Then tragedy struck. We never knew how the fire started, but it happened on a night when we were closed for minor repairs. I was woken in the middle of the night by a call from my security guard telling me that the Teatro was on fire. It was horrific, Mr. Senn! When Stephan and I reached the Teatro, the fire was blazing out of every window!" Mia had to stop talking and let the torturous image pass through her mind.

Mia became agitated as she said, "The fire brigade was late to arrive. We could have saved most of the place if they had shown up on time."

Mia paused and sighed again. "But the Teatro was in flames. The stage was completely burnt. It was catastrophic."

Mia's fired eyes stared at Senn as she continued, "When we tried to claim insurance, we found that our policy had lapsed. It was a hopeless time." Mia paused and took a big gulp to finish her second glass of chardonnay.

Senn was starting to get a better picture of Mia's predicament now.

Mia dabbed her red lipstick softly before speaking, "We were broke. We had no money to restore the Teatro and owed the bank a lot for our expensive productions."

Mia's choked voice had lowered to a rasp as she continued, "We were so desperate, one night Stephan suggested we run away from Venice to escape the banks. And then Angelo called." Mia held her head in her hand as she recounted the call. "He sounded Sicilian and was very kind and said he was sending us some figs from his orchards in Albania and wanted us to try them and hung up. I had no idea who he was or what to expect."

Mia frowned as she continued talking (now much more animatedly). "The next morning, we had a knock on our door, and standing outside was a short, middle-aged, bald man, and behind him was a pickup truck full of crates. Loaded with figs!"

Mia's eyes caught something outside that made her nervousness reappear. A boat had pulled up in the square outside, and some men were laughing loudly while moving furniture into a house. Senn could tell her jitters were resurfacing.

Mia recovered her focus and continued, "Stephan and the man spoke for a few minutes, and then he parked the truck in the alley and left. Stephan later told me that the man worked for the local Venetian mafia boss Angelo. Seemingly, they wanted to help us restore the Teatro as Angelo's deceased mother was very fond of the Teatro, and Angelo himself loved visiting the Rossi when he was a kid."

Mia stopped, stared frustratedly at Senn, and said, "We had a hard choice, Mr. Senn. To leave Venice or take help from the mafia. I asked Stephan to meet them and understand what they wanted in exchange."

Mia took another gulp of her wine and continued, "He met them a day later. It was a bizarre meeting! They blindfolded him throughout the meeting, so he never saw anyone. Later, Stephan came back and told me that in exchange, they wanted us to let them have access to the basement of the Teatro for *storage.*"

Senn nodded.

"So for the last two years, we've regularly received a loan from a private money lender to pay for the restoration, and in return, we stay away from the basement," Mia said with a shrug.

Then she looked out at the shimmering canal, and wistfully said, "I wish we had sold the Teatro, left Venice, and not done the deal with the devil."

Senn could tell Mia was full of remorse and wanted out. But there was something he wanted to clarify. Puzzled, he asked, "But how do they access the basement without anyone noticing?"

Mia lowered her voice. "They use an underground bridge under the canal connecting a house opposite the Teatro basement. Luca has the key to the private mooring spot to enter the Teatro. In the 19th century, a mini theatre was attached to the Teatro for private performances for the rich and infamous. During the second World War, the tunnel was active among the resistance movement, but we closed it decades ago. The mafia came and reopened it during the restoration."

Senn listened intently, amazed at what he was hearing. Mia was spilling the beans on the Venetian mafia's operations under the Teatro for the first time to anyone and trying to extricate herself from their control. He couldn't decide if she was brave or stupid. But he was sure of one thing: she was terrified for her and her son's life. So every word was untarnished and unvarnished.

Senn waited as Mia gulped some more wine and then asked the question still on his mind, "And what about the picture? Why are the mafia sending you that, and why now?"

Mia froze and had a pleading look, begging Senn not to ask that question. She leaned back on her chair, closed her eyes, and rocked her body as she prayed silently.

Then after a few seconds of silence whispered in a trembling voice, "They know about my daughter."

Senn's eyes widened. But he let her explain.

Mia lowered her head and spoke in a haunted voice. "Mr. Senn, my mother died giving birth to me in 1962 on a cruise ship. My father had already died a few months earlier. Moments before dying, my mother told her roommate to warn me about the Conti curse when I grew up."

Mia paused, looked down at her graceful, gem-encrusted fingers, and continued, "She told her that our family has a curse. If a girl is born, the infant dies, or the mother dies. Just like my mother did and what happened to my grandmother."

Senn sat in silence as Mia confessed. He could feel she was revealing something dark and profound as a way of atonement.

She sounded pretty detached as she continued, "When I was 19, I had a secret affair with a local mafia boss who was much older than me but loved me. He was delighted to hear I was pregnant; we knew it was a girl. But I was scared and ashamed. I was so confused about becoming a mother. My mother's warning kept playing in my head. I could not face anyone, so I moved into the basement of the Teatro for the last weeks of the pregnancy and avoided everyone until I gave birth."

Mia struggled to continue talking as her tears rose. "My daughter was born at midnight. She had the biggest blue eyes I had ever seen in my life. She was an angel."

Mia stared blankly and said, "But I covered her eyes with a sheet and choked her."

Still staring blankly, Mia took a sip of her wine, wrung her hands, and said, "I was terrified of the curse and couldn't ever have a child again. So I secretly adopted Stephan from a passing gypsy troupe."

Mia paused, stared at Senn, and said, "And the mafia knows this because the woman on the cruise ship with my mother that night was Sophia, Angelo's mother."

Senn was speechless.

So the wailing ghost in the Teatro was Mia's slain daughter. And Mia, her killer.

CHAPTER 27

THE LINGERING FOG OF DEATH

The waiter brought their espresso macchiato and started chatting with Senn while Mia went to use the washroom. The waiter from Naples complained about how much he missed the women back home and how Venetian women were not his type. Senn enjoyed the light-hearted banter and laughed at his jokes until a blood-chilling scream rang out from the far end of the restaurant.

Senn jumped out of his chair, sprinted past the shocked guests and servers, and saw the cries coming from the ladies' washroom. He burst in to see a young woman standing outside one of the toilets hysterically screaming, covering her face with her hands.

Senn grabbed the door handle and yanked it open. His jaw dropped in horror.

Hanging from the ceiling lamp from a nylon rope was the lifeless body of Mia, eyes closed, neck tilted at an acute angle. Senn jumped up on the sink, unhooked the rope, and grabbed Mia's drooping shoulders as they collapsed in a heap in his arms. He loosened the noose around her neck, gently lowered her to the ground, and looked for a pulse.

There was none.

Senn tried to resuscitate Mia with CPR. Even though her body was still warm, he was not getting much reaction from her collapsed lungs. A hushed crowd had gathered around Senn and Mia as they watched him trying to revive her. The restaurant manager shouted that the ambulance was on its way along with the police. Some of the staff who knew Mia well were crying.

After a couple of minutes, Senn stopped performing CPR, gently lifted her arms, and crossed them over her body. Her cheeks had turned a crimson pink with a few blisters under her eyes due to the asphyxiation, but her face looked eerily calm and serene.

Senn picked himself up and stepped away from the body as the police sirens got louder. The ambulance arrived on the scene, the medics rushed past Senn, and the police entered soon after. The mayhem had attracted the entire square's attention, including the tourist-packed canal boats. Senn stepped outside to get some air and regain his composure.

His initial shock was slowly crumbling into sadness. He felt heavy-hearted that Mia was unable to escape her misfortune. He could still hear her distressed voice ringing in his ears. Senn felt sorry for her violent demise and guilty that he'd failed to protect her from her assailants. He was particularly disgusted by how she'd been impudently intimidated and brutally assassinated in broad daylight. He was sure that her stalker had something to do with Mia's death. Senn scanned the faces in the crowd to see if he could spot the man, but there was no one he recognized.

Amid all the mayhem, Senn heard his phone ring. It was Anna.

Senn answered to hear her breathless, anxious voice on the other end.

"Senn, please come to the Teatro immediately. The police have discovered a body in the canal." Then after a pause, she said, "It's badly burnt but belongs to a woman. The police want you to identify if it's Laura."

Senn felt choked as his fists clenched in dread. "I'm on my way," he added, "I have bad news. Mia's dead."

Anna uttered a loud groan. "What! When?"

"A few minutes ago," Senn replied. "I was having lunch with her when it happened. Someone strangled and hung her in the washroom." Senn paused and said, "I think it's the same man who attacked me."

Anna fell silent, then said worriedly, "Get off the phone and get here soon. You could be in danger."

Senn nodded and disconnected. He knew he was now a marked man. Mia's confessions had turned him from an inconsequential, pesky investigator at best into a full-blown operational threat for the mafia.

But all he could think about right then was the identity of the discovered body. He desperately hoped it was not Laura.

Senn turned to look towards the restaurant for a final time. As the slanting rays of the winter sun cracked through the clouds and cast long shadows on the ashen tiles, the medics parted the crowds carrying the white sheet-wrapped body of Mia on a stretcher past him into the waiting ambulance.

Senn informed the police of his destination and left.

Arriving twenty minutes later at the Teatro, Senn spotted Anna at the entrance of the cordoned-off square on the phone, talking agitatedly to someone. She looked angry as she shook her hands wildly with a deep jagged frown across her face. As soon as she spotted Senn, she disconnected the phone, walked up to him with a concerned look, and raised the police tape for him to enter the restricted area. Anna introduced Senn to the attending police officers who led the way to the body.

She darted an anxious glance at Senn and said, "It's a gruesome sight. The body's been in the water for at least a week. They found it because it got caught in a Vaporetto's propeller and jammed it."

Senn nodded grimly, but his hands were shaking. He'd seen decomposed bodies before, but this one was blood numbing.

The Campo San Barnaba lay exhumed of its tourists, and a large tugboat held up a red crane dredging the water. The body covered by a bright yellow tarp was on the steps leading up to the square from the canal.

Senn grudgingly approached the suffocating stench of the covered corpse and steadied himself for the confrontation. The medic removed the cover to reveal a young blonde woman's heavily bloated and burnt, naked body. The body was torn and lacerated across her neck and arms, and there were multiple stab wounds on her chest and stomach. Whoever killed her had subjected her to frenzied and savage torture before setting her ablaze.

Senn shook his head in disbelief and confirmed it was not Laura.

Senn walked away, shaken but relieved, and joined Anna, talking to some officers. He again confirmed it was not Laura to Anna and the officers present.

Anna, looking relieved, said, "Thank god it's not Laura! I wasn't sure. How did you know for sure?"

"Laura has a tattoo of a bird flying out of a cage on her shoulders. This woman had none. I was with her when she got that tattoo in Prague."

With a big sigh, Anna smiled. "Sweet."

Senn looked sadly at Anna and said, "But my bird is still caged, and I can't find her."

CHAPTER 28

STEPHAN SWEARS OUT LIES

"Men in rage strike those that wish them best."

—WILLIAM SHAKESPEARE

Stephan wept hopelessly, holding Mia's hands as her body lay on the coroner's investigation table, awaiting an inquest while Anna and Senn stood outside with the police. Colonel Taino was also present and getting debriefed by his team.

The courtyard outside the coroner's office was jam-packed with media teams with cameras and equipment frenetically speculating and reporting Mia's brutal assassination. The press had a field day connecting Mia and Stephan's recent drug smuggling accusations to her violent death. All fingers were pointing at the mafia for carrying out the assassination.

Col. Taino walked up to Anna and Senn and, addressing Senn, inquired, "Did you get a good look at the man who attacked you? We have received a file of pictures of some mafia men operating in this area that I want to show you because we might be looking for the same man for both crimes."

Senn was unsure about the man's specific features but wanted to see if anyone in the line-up came close. The officer's computer screen showed many men whose ages ranged from teenagers to grey and middle-aged convicts or ex-convicts. Senn remembered the man's most striking features, *the mocking, amused look in his hooded, grey eyes and stained teeth.* None of the men fitted his mental image.

Just then, Senn heard steps from behind the coroner's office, and the door swung open, and a troubled, disheveled Stephan appeared while being consoled by the coroner's nurse. He stopped and stared at the multitude waiting for him like a startled cat.

When he saw the police officers, his eyes caught fire, and rage swept through his veins. He walked up to the colonel, raised his fist, and started shouting at him and blaming him for the death of his mother. The police officers around the Col. immediately stepped in and blocked Stephan's aggressive advances. He kept shouting,

"You're murderers, you're murderers," as the Colonel tried to reason with him to calm down.

Stephan looked in utter despair with sporadic convulsions of rage and tears. After a few seconds of struggle with the police officers, his knees buckled, and he fell to the floor and lay there crying out, "Oh, Mama, Mama!" inconsolably.

Some of the press in the room pointed their cameras and microphones at this heart-wrenching display of grief and broadcast it live on various social media and T.V. channels.

Senn couldn't help but feel pity for Stephan. Even though not his own, Mia was more than a mother to him. She was his friend, manager, and guide and guarded him against the press and their barbs about his oppressive and grueling methods of treating his actors and actresses during rehearsals. She was his world.

Stephan calmed down after a few seconds, stood, did a chameleon-like volte-face, extended his hand, and apologized to the colonel for his harsh words. He walked calmly to his boat, past the hordes of crazed paparazzi that flooded him with questions, cameras, and microphones, and drove off.

Colonel Taino smirked as the boat disappeared around the corner. "Stephan is the world's most crooked actor."

Senn slanted his eyebrows with a questioning look at the colonel, wondering what he meant by that cryptic comment.

Taino calmly replied, "I spoke to him yesterday. He's still denying any mafia involvement in the Teatro. He's adamant that there was no deal with the mafia or Teatro drug smuggling."

Senn, surprised, said, "But Mia confessed everything to me. There's a secret passage in the basement where the drugs are loaded and shifted. She even said Stephan met a mafia boss called Angelo to finalize this collaboration. The key I found in Luca's house might be for this secret passage."

Taino listened intently at Senn, and slowly his eyes lit up. "Then, for god's sake, let's go and find this tunnel and bust Stephan's lies once and for all."

The irritated colonel stormed out of the coroner's office and jumped into his boat along with Senn and Anna. They reached the Teatro in a few minutes.

Led by Col. Taino and a few officers, they entered the empty house opposite the Teatro, went down to the basement, and found a metal door. Senn tried Luca's key, which opened into a dimly lit passage over the canal, which led to a private mooring point attached to the wall of the Teatro, big enough to fit a couple of boats.

Senn scanned the space, looked across at the colonel and said, "This is where they must be loading the drugs from the Teatro, and they must have abducted Laura from as well."

The colonel and Anna nodded in agreement.

But they noticed another door leading into the Teatro, which was locked. The only way in was from inside the Teatro.

The colonel ordered for the door to be broken open. His officers got to work and, within minutes, had wrenched the door apart. The instant they opened the door and descended the steps, the officer in the front jerked to a halt.

The Teatro basement was flooded waist-deep in water. All the broken furniture and equipment were underwater or floating on top, making it impossible to move further. Whatever game Stephan was playing, it was certainly not a shallow one.

CHAPTER 29

THE STALKER'S ON THE PROWL

"Color is my daylong obsession, joy, and torment."

—CLAUDE MONET

Senn restlessly rechecked his phone with his pruney fingers as he lay sunken in his scalding hot bathtub back in his attic--his last refuge to fathom conundrums.

In the distant San Marco square, the clock tower chimed midnight as the gusty, cold wind picked up a notch and whistled through cracks in the bathroom window. It had been twelve days since Laura went missing, and Senn felt torturously separated from knowing her whereabouts.

He'd tantalizingly lost her trail on Lido Island.

He'd just finished re-reading the police forensic reports (for the third time) with its incredible findings.

First off, it confirmed Laura *was* in Luca's boat, *but the DNA in the warehouse did not belong to her but matched the burnt corpse under the Teatro.* The woman's identity was still a mystery. She had Eastern European roots without any criminal records.

This discovery shocked Senn, but he also felt relieved that Laura wasn't tortured.

But this made Senn wonder if Laura was ever in the warehouse and if Luca or Dario had ever met her. There was no direct evidence linking Laura to the men.

The only person who definitely met Laura was Stephan.

The second shocker was the discovery of *two* additional sets of fingerprints in the warehouse, and one of them was a woman. The man had traces of cocaine on his fingers. The frustrating part was that the new DNA and prints were faint and did not conclusively match any known criminal in their database.

This evidence suggested that Luca and Dario knew these two people and knew about the warehouse's Eastern European woman.

And finally, the report did confirm Luca and Dario's fingerprints and DNA on the boat and the warehouse; however, results from Luca's and Dario's houses and the car had proved inconclusive.

The devil was still evasive with its impressions.

Senn hoped the forensic results on Luca, Mia, or Dario's bodies had embalmed the scent of the devil.

So, unless Senn could quickly dig out something new, Laura's trail had frustratingly gone cold again.

Senn grabbed the towel from the heated rack as he stepped out of the tub, wiped himself dry, and looked out of his fourth-floor porthole window at the gelid canal below.

Senn's eyes narrowed as he spotted a police boat moored in the canal and two officers inside sharing a smoke. He quickly switched off the apartment lights and continued to watch the men. No one had informed him about receiving any escort or security. The boat looked old and rickety but with clear blue-and-white police markings across the port and hull.

Wide awake and alert, Senn redressed into jeans and jumper, clipped his push dagger under his belt, and watched for movements in the boat. Occasionally one of the men would look up at his studio window while smoking a cigarette.

On the spur, Senn decided to investigate these men further. He quickly texted Anna, asking if she knew anything about being allocated a police escort. Zipping his hoodie, Senn reckoned that if they were legitimate cops, it would clear his doubt instantly. If not, he intended to get some answers about who they were and why they were stalking his place in the middle of the night in a fake police boat!

Senn walked down the creaking steps to the ground floor, unlocked the main door, confidently stepped out, and stared straight into the eyes of the men parked on the opposite side of the canal. Startled by Senn's sudden appearance, the men watched steely eyed as Senn walked down the sidewalk towards the small brick bridge to cross over to their side. Senn did not know what to expect. But in his pocket, he held his unsheathed push dagger, ready to strike if he felt any threat.

The boat and its occupants made no sudden moves. Senn walked up and stood on the side outside facing the men and said, "Good evening, officers."

One of the bald, bearded men nodded in acknowledgment. "Good evening Mr. Senn. A bit too cold to be out and about?"

Surprised and relieved to hear his name, Senn smiled. "I was about to ask you the same thing."

The man smiled back and said, "Col. Taino sent us to keep an eye on your house tonight."

Senn reassured but now curious, asked, "Wow! But what's the hurry because no one told me about this?"

In a more severe tone, the man fell silent, stepped out of the boat, and, accompanied by his almost twin-looking partner, replied, "You better go back home. It's not safe for you to be out here tonight."

Confounded by the urgency in the officer's voice, Senn repeated his question, to which the man put his hand out in a halting gesture and, in a calm but cold tone, ordered, "Mr. Senn, please. Let me walk you back."

Senn felt the firm push from the man behind his back as he escorted Senn back across the bridge to his front door while the other man walked a few steps behind.

Senn reached his front door, smiled, and thanked the plain-clothed officers before closing the door behind him.

That was a bad idea, Senn thought as he sprinted back to his flat and turned the key. He pulled out his phone and saw Anna had replied to his text.

The message read, "Yes, they want you dead."

CHAPTER 30

"I THINK YOU SHOULD LEAVE VENICE."

"Well, I am not afraid of the humans,
but of what is inhuman in them."

—IVO ANDRIC

Col. Taino paced his office, wearing a birthday boy paper hat shouting expletives on the phone to some poor sod. At the same time, Senn sat a few feet away, pouring over the messages intercepted from the Venetian mafia on the Tor network's dark web.

The messages were all in a Venetian dialect of Italian and written in cryptic anagrams and sent from someone named *Izanami to Corus.* The Italian police had been tracking a few Onion sites on the dark web for cocaine trafficking in the Venice area and were alerted when they saw Senn's name pop up on the message board of a well-known hit man named Corus.

The section that Col. Taino had highlighted for Senn was the exchange of messages between Izanami and Corus in the last 12 hours that mentioned his name numerous times.

Taino finished his call, sat, grabbed Senn's arm, squeezed it tightly, and said, "I think you should get out of Venice for a while, Senn. This Corus guy is the Venetian mafia's go-to hitman when they want to target a foreigner, and he's talking about you in the last few hours. The last time this message board got active was a year ago when a foreign investigative journalist like you had come to Venice trying to find stolen artifacts, and he, like the art, sadly went missing. We still have no idea what happened to him. But my team spotted the same discussion between these two people."

On the printouts, Senn could see Corus had acknowledged a string of messages from Izanami that clearly said Senn was becoming a problem and needed some attention. The police had highlighted three comments from Izanami to Corus that stated Senn was now a marked man. Taino pointed out how the anagram dispersed Senn's name between the operative keywords.

troppns enas (Senn knows too much)

oramandare a ncsenasa (Senn needs to go home.)

Collannas peer (necklace for Senn)

Senn took a deep breath and nodded. This was not the first time he'd been threatened or targeted in his career. He couldn't say he was used to it, but he knew why the people threatening him did that.

Because they were scared he was flying too close to the truth. They were scared he had figured out too much too fast. It was when they brought out the scare tactic to deter him from coming any closer.

But even though he felt fear, there was no way he would leave.

Senn clenched his jaw and shook his head as he addressed the colonel. "Sir, they want me out of Venice, but I can't leave without Laura."

Taino tried to reason with Senn and even hinted at *throwing him out of the country* for his safety but quieted when he saw Senn was adamant.

Senn raised his head and saw Anna walk in (a bit late as usual). Taino gave her a beaming smile, got up, and gave her a big hug. Anna smiled and kissed him on both his cheeks. Senn could see how much Taino adored his protege crime buster niece.

She looked stunning in her buff pink woolen jumper under a black leather jacket and jeans. Senn noticed she had a new set of black boots with silver studded stars all over the ankle. Her hair was tied up in a loose bun, revealing her long, slender neck.

She sat next to Senn and greeted him with a big grin as he handed her a cup of freshly brewed coffee. Senn glanced at her neck and spotted small blood clots and scratches that ran up and down on both sides of her neck, which she lightly rubbed as she read the compilation of the message boards between *Izanami and Corus.* In addition, she had a small bandage on her wrist that she tried to keep covered under her jumper.

Anna noticed Senn's glances at her bandage and remarked, "I had a cat emergency this morning. I picked him up this morning as usual, and he attacked me. I was so shocked! But then I noticed he had bruises on his back. I rushed him to the vet and found a shoulder fracture."

"Ouch!" shouted Taino as he had Senn exchanged a pained expression sympathizing for Anna.

"Good lord, who did that to him?" asked Taino.

"Another tom cat, probably," replied a calm Anna. "It's mating season, and these male cats get very aggressive."

Senn smirked and, in jest, said, "Like Corus and Izanami."

Not seeing the joke, Anna replied severely, "These messages are deadly serious, Senn. They are after you. You should stay low and maybe even leave Venice for a while. We can keep you updated on the phone. Please don't take this lightly."

Senn shook his head. "I know these threats are not hollow, but I can't leave without Laura, Anna. I know she's alive, and we are close."

As she crossed her arms, Anna still looked concerned and protested, "But we've hit a dead end."

Senn disagreed, "We know Stephan's lying. We might know where Laura is if we can get him to talk."

Taino chipped in, "I agree with Senn; Stephan is our prime suspect now, but he's refusing to talk until we can find something substantial connecting him to the drugs or Laura's abduction. The search for the tunnel was futile. We found nothing, and now he's rallying public sympathy for himself as the harassed victim of police brutality. He's hiding something sinister. I know it. But I can't put my finger on it," Taino said as he slammed his fist on the veneered oak table.

Senn nodded in frustration.

The slippery Stephan was the prime suspect. Again.

CHAPTER 31

STEPHAN A THIEF OR MUCH WORSE?

Senn was at the door, leaving Taino's office, when he remembered something and turned his head and shouted, "Happy birthday and anniversary, Colonel! Don't forget to open the present we bought you." Senn winked at Anna as she'd arranged to get Taino's favorite rum chocolates as a joint present.

Anna smiled back at Senn, waved Taino a flying kiss, and stepped out of the police station in the drizzling rain. Anna pulled her hoodie over her head and gave Senn a searching look. "Wanna grab a drink?"

"Sure," replied Senn as they ran across the square into a bar.

Anna chose a seat by the window overlooking the empty square facing the police station and ordered a glass of red wine. Senn did the same as he sat, placed his backpack on the chair next to him, and pulled out his laptop to review his notes from the meeting.

Senn re-read Col. Taino's confirmation that the police had searched Stephan's house once but found nothing that could implicate him in the drug trafficking charges. He reiterated that Stephan had denied any connection to the mafia and blamed the drug discovery on his boat on Luca's underworld activities. He had also vigorously distanced himself from Luca by claiming Luca was an old employee whom they treated as a friend and knew nothing about his mafia connections.

Senn turned to Anna and asked, "Did you know the journalist who went missing a year ago was looking for a stolen Modigliani?"

"No, I didn't know that."

Senn showed her the YouTube news clip that reported the incident and the young British journalist doing an interview where he said he was looking for stolen artworks that routed via Venice on their way to private art galleries around the world.

The journalist theorized that the mafia was stealing and selling them off in underground auctions, earning them millions. At the end of the interview, the reporter asked him which painter's work was the most stolen and trafficked by the mafia, and the journalist smiled and replied, "Modigliani."

Anna's eyes widened as Senn paused the video and continued.

"Yesterday, I found a Sotheby's list of all the stolen paintings of Modigliani. Do you remember when Stephan chased us out of the basement the first time; I saw a portrait of a woman stashed amongst the stuff there that looked a lot like one of these missing Modigliani's."

Senn lowered his voice and said, "I think Stephan's real passion is selling stolen art from the Teatro. The drugs are a sideshow that he can't help but allow the mafia to peddle because he needs them to do his dirty business."

Anna looked studiously at Senn. "And Laura found the stolen painting?"

Senn nodded. "She was a fine art major from Oxford. She had a deep knowledge of Italian renaissance painters, and if she'd found a Modigliani stashed in the basement, she would have asked Stephan about it."

Senn continued, "I watched a video where Stephan was doing a zoom interview from his house. On his wall in the distance was another painting resembling a stolen Modigliani. He loves the painter's work so much that he displays it proudly and thinks people won't notice."

Senn leaned forward and whispered, "I think if we can catch Stephan displaying stolen art on his wall, we can get him to confess his mafia involvement and tell us where he's hiding, Laura."

"Do you still think Laura's alive?" Anna asked, looking a little sympathetically at Senn.

"Yes," replied Senn. "I know it in my heart."

Senn was gulping down the last sip of his wine when the square rocked with a loud explosion that shook the bar's windows and shattered the glass of the building opposite them. Anna gasped, shot out of her chair, and ran out of the bar screaming.

Senn took a second to realize that the loud explosion had come out of the police station, and the thick, black smoke rising from the first-floor window of the building was the office of Col. Taino!

CHAPTER 32

"IS HE DEAD?"

Anna sobbed uncontrollably in Senn's arms as flames engulfed Col. Taino's office.

Wailing sirens of armored police boats crammed the canals as officers shouted at pedestrians and tourists to move out of the square or stay indoors. Emergency services rushed in and out of the smoldering building carrying the injured and burnt victims out. Terrified residents peeped out from behind their curtains, clutching their children tightly.

Thick, black smoke billowed out of Col. Taino's office as four fire engines worked relentlessly to douse the blaze and prevent it from spreading to the whole square.

Senn watched agog at the unfolding carnage. He couldn't believe the deafening explosion had emanated from Col Taino's office and turned into a ball of flame, ravaging his office instantly. Luckily the fire brigade was next door and arrived on the scene within a few minutes. But the fire had spread fast to the floors above and started to move east in the wind direction. As Senn looked at the charred remains of the colonel's smoldering office, he feared for Taino's life and prayed that he was unhurt and the explosion was not an act of arson.

Overcome by the trauma and smoke, Anna started to faint and complained to Senn about feeling dizzy. Senn grabbed a medic passing by and asked for help. The nurses noticing Anna's state put her into a wheelchair, placed an oxygen mask over her head, and whisked her to one of the ambulance boats in front of them. Senn anxiously followed them and waited outside.

Amid the chaos, Senn's eye caught an irate seagull squawking loudly and swooping down at something on one of the rooftops. He had seen seagulls do this as protective behavior toward their chicks. But his curiosity turned to alarm when he noticed a man standing on a narrow terrace holding a pair of binoculars, looking at the square and trying to scare the bird away simultaneously.

Senn let out a gasp as a shiver went down his spine. He instantly recognized the tall, lanky man as his attacker and stalker, Mia's stalker, and possibly her murderer.

Senn had to act fast.

He ducked behind an advertising boarding and ran down the hallway towards the man's building while covering his face with his bag. He ran along the wall, hiding from the line of sight of the man's binoculars until he was right under the house where the man was standing.

Senn looked up to check if he was still there and was startled to see the man staring right down at him from the attic window. They faced off for a second, uncertain how to act, and then the man locked eyes with Senn, gave him a mocking laugh, showed him his middle finger, and disappeared over the roof to the back of the house.

Senn tried to chase but saw the man jumping from one roof to another over the narrow alleys between each house. His long legs carried him effortlessly over rooftops like an expert traceur. Within seconds, he disappeared into the forested concrete labyrinth of Venice.

Senn couldn't help but be impressed at the man's parkour skill. He seemed to glide over the roofs as if on a magic carpet. The fact that he was observing the square gave enough ammo for Senn to believe that he had something to do with the explosion.

This time Senn had got a good look at the man.

He matched Mia's description of menacing grey, hooded eyes, hollow cheeks, and a long, hooked, aquiline nose resembling a belligerent Daniel Day-Lewis in *Gangs of New York*.

Senn turned around and ran back to Anna's ambulance to find she was still inside. Police and paramilitary had swarmed into the area, pushing everyone to empty the square. Recognizing Captain Mikkey in the crowd, Senn shouted, asking about the colonel's whereabouts, and got a blank response suggesting he was not sure.

The media teams had lined the yellow-taped cordon with their equipment and microphones and started reporting the scene with the smoldering office of the colonel as a macabre backdrop.

The sun was starting to set, and the biting cold wind ruffled Senn's curly hair and quickly dried his sweaty brow as his eyes darted anxiously, searching for a word from Anna and how the colonel was doing.

Senn's phone lit up with Anna calling.

Anna sounded joyous as she said, "Senn, Uncle's alive! Thank god, thank god, thank god. He's alive."

Senn almost collapsed in relief.

"Wow! that's amazing, Anna," Senn replied. "That's just amazing. Did you speak to him? What happened?"

Anna sounded breathless and worried as she spoke, "No. But I talked to one of the officers who told me it was a bomb. They don't know the details yet, but it went off when the colonel was in the toilet. The door saved him. He could escape from the skylight before the whole office caught fire. He told me he's now in a secret bunker. "

Senn listened, grim and attentive.

Anna continued, "I'm scared, Senn. The mafia used to operate like this a few years ago when they wanted to take revenge or silence someone who knew too much."

Senn and Anna knew the colonel was leading the crusade against the rising tide of cocaine and heroin making its way into Venice from neighboring countries.

He'd busted a significant shipment of a tonne of cocaine a few weeks ago that had made headlines all over the country. It was one of the biggest crackdowns in Europe in the last decade. The mafia was hurting, and this sounded like a case of drastic action on their part to get even.

Anna sobbed as she continued, "Uncle Taino is a good man and does not deserve this. I am so worried. Do you think our case has something to do with this?"

Senn thought for a moment and considered if he should tell her about his meeting with the stalker and then said, "I don't know, Anna. The people we're dealing with are ruthless and will stop at nothing to get their way."

Then Senn paused and asked, "Are you OK? How are you feeling?"

Anna told him she was feeling better but was heading home to rest, said goodbye, and hung up. Senn hung up and gave a big sigh of relief. He had held back from telling Anna about the stalker because he didn't want to worry her. She needed to get some rest after such a traumatic shock.

CHAPTER 33

ESCAPING THE CLAWS OF VENICE

"To escape from the world means that one's mind is not concerned with the opinions of the world."

—DŌGEN

Senn walked briskly to the Teatro, hoping to talk to Stephan and clear something vital, but found it locked with a notice stating the house was mourning Mia's death, and all rehearsals and tourist visits remained canceled until further notice.

A radiant picture of a smiling Mia hung on the door, and condolence messages, bouquets, and candles piled up on the floor.

Senn read some of the messages that lamented her death and said they loved her, missed her, and wished her peace in heaven. An old lady walked past him and kissed Mia's picture, while a young girl who accompanied her laid a wreath of white roses on the floor. Mia was a vibrant part of the local community, and her sudden and violent demise had touched the hearts of Venetians, young and old.

Senn was about to leave when he noticed the service door of the Teatro open, and a tall man emerged, walking briskly down the sidewalk past the square heading west. He wore a dark blue overcoat, had a flowing, grey beard, shoulder-length, grey hair, and retro, tortoise horn-rimmed glasses.

In spite of the impressive makeup and hair, the man carried the same slight limp on the left leg as Stephan did when he was in a hurry, piquing Senn's suspicions to follow him. The man walked briskly along the canal promenade for a few hundred meters and disappeared behind the private side garden door of Hotel Palazzo Foscari, confirming it was Stephan.

Senn knew from his research that Mia and Stephan owned the penthouse apartment on the fifth floor of the five-star hotel facing the Grand Canal.

It was about 6 PM, and on a hunch, Senn walked into a small bar outside the hotel, ordered a beer, and waited to see if Stephan would re-emerge.

Senn was glad to get a few minutes of rest. It had been one hell of a day. The deadly attempt on Col. Taino's life and coming face to face with his stalker at the police station had rattled Senn considerably.

Senn had considered lying low and maybe even leaving Venice for a while, but that would have only meant one thing—letting Laura down. Senn was no quitter.

And what he had found early this morning potentially changed the course of his entire investigation.

While rummaging for the umpteenth time through Laura's things, he found a tantalizing clue.

Wrapped in a paper bag, tucked inside a discreet flap of her makeup bag, was a silver box with a small Teatro Rossi insignia engraved on one side. Inside was a gold bracelet and a card with the handwritten words, *Be my forever.*

It looked like a romantic gift from Stephan to Laura.

Although Laura had never uttered a word about seeing anyone, let alone Stephan, Senn was surprised by the care with which the box was hidden and preserved in her bag.

This clue was potentially a game changer for the course of Senn's entire investigation.

Because this meant Stephan was protecting Laura, not harming her.

It fundamentally pivoted the whole investigation in favor of Stephan.

And Laura was just a victim of being at the wrong time and place.

Senn reimagined that Laura must have seen something in the basement, and the mafia wanted to get rid of her. And Stephan protected her.

And now he was being blackmailed by the mafia to reveal her location. But he was holding out and hoped to negotiate her freedom. But Stephan had underestimated their serious intent, and when they killed Mia, he went on the run with Laura.

Senn could acutely feel Stephan's dilemma: to protect Laura and risk his life or sacrifice her in return for his safety.

Senn did not have time to suggest this hypothesis to Anna and Taino.

He hoped to speak to Stephan and see his reaction first.

He hoped Stephan would open up and agree that he was protecting and hiding Laura from the rampant mafia so that he could help them. But Senn also knew that Stephan was frightened by his mother's assassination and unprepared to trust anyone in the current climate.

He just needed to speak to Stephan.

Senn had just taken his first sip of the beer when the garden gate of the hotel opened, and the bearded man walked out with a backpack slung over his shoulder and headed out to the canal. Senn hurriedly left a five euro note under the chilled glass of beer and rushed out of the bar in hot pursuit of the man who headed east and ducked around the tourists lining the streets.

Senn had no time to cross over to the other side, so he ran along the opposite side of the canal, trying to keep the man in sight. At one point, a sailboat obstructed his view for a few seconds, and when the boat passed, the man had disappeared. Senn ran to the next bridge along the canal, raced to the other side, and tried to spot the man again, but it looked like he had lost him. Frustrated and angry at himself, Senn walked along the busy streets, looking into bars and brightly lit shops selling all kinds of Venetian memorabilia to smiling, giggly tourists.

Senn paused to catch his breath and calm his paranoia. The adrenaline rush slowly turned to dread as Senn desperately looked for Stephan in the maze of a busy Venetian evening.

A Vaporetto departed from one station and headed towards St. Macro square. From the corner of his eye, Senn spotted Stephan sitting with his backpack over his lap, staring cautiously at the darkness outside. He looked worried and preoccupied.

Senn started running. He knew the next stop and could arrive at the same time as the boat if he sprinted.

By the time Senn reached St. Marco square, the Vaporetto had departed from the station, but Stephan was still inside.

The boat's next and final destination was Lido Island.

Senn jumped into a vacant taxi parked on the water and asked the captain to take him to the island but keep the Vaporetto in sight as one of his friends was on it. The captain was in a festive mood and turned up the radio playing songs from the disco era, and Senn endured the captain doing his karaoke overlays of "Dancing Queen" by Abba and Boney M's "Rasputin".

When Senn stepped onto the island after shaking the Captain's hand and complementing his soprano voice, the Vaparetto had docked, and Stephan had stepped out and headed towards the underground car park.

Senn sneaked in from one of the broken side glass doors and saw Stephan opening his Maserati, throwing his bags inside, and starting the car.

Senn needed a car to follow. He scanned the parking lot and saw an old, dusty Fiat Cinquecento in a corner. Senn unzipped the small shoulder pocket in his jacket, removed his lock-picking wire, and managed to unlock the car door within seconds.

It looked like an early '90s model, and he hoped his hot-wiring technique would work. He inserted his flat metal wire into the ignition and pushed it hard until it reached the end of the ignition cylinder. Then he slowly turned it like a key. After a few tries, the car fired to life.

The car's fuel tank was almost empty, but everything seemed to work. Senn turned the headlights on, engaged the gears, and drove the car up the ramp. And as he exited, he spotted Stephan's car turn the corner and speed off into the distance heading south toward Alberoni.

CHAPTER 34

STEPHAN BRAVES THE STORM

"But I know, somehow, that only when it is dark enough can you see the stars."

—MARTIN LUTHER KING, JR.

Senn's Cinquecento swerved and skidded in the blustery wind as he tried to keep up with Stephan's Maserati down Via Alberoni on Lido Island.

The rain lashed the windscreens, making it treacherous to drive without wipers, which were unfortunately missing. Senn was grateful for the lack of traffic on the road as he floored the accelerator and drove by instinct down the skinny island main road.

He desperately hoped Stephan was leading him to Laura.

The shocking discovery of the bracelet and the letter had stumped Senn. It was a closely guarded secret between the couple, maybe due to their professional working relationship or their twenty-year age difference.

Or maybe because Stephan did not want Mia to know. Senn had read media stories speculating Mia was highly possessive of her son and frowned on any woman getting too close to him.

Senn slowed as the road reached a roundabout. Stephan was nowhere in sight. One road continued south to the warehouse and the lighthouse facing the ocean, and the other headed to the jetty, looking into the lagoon. He had to choose which way to proceed. Senn nervously looked at the fuel gauge car, which showed empty. The rain was still hammering down hard over the thin, rusted roof of the battered vehicle. He was running out of options.

Senn chose the warehouse, expecting Stephan to try to escape through the cave. All lights were off as Senn slowly approached the building with no sign of Stephan's car. Senn continued slowly for a few hundred meters until the dead end behind the lighthouse. Apart from some flapping metal roofing that had come unhinged, the place was like a silent cemetery.

Senn turned the car and retraced his way to the roundabout towards the jetty as he kicked himself for losing Stephan's trail.

After a few hundred meters of driving, the tar road morphed into a gravel path, and Senn had to slow down as the car lurched over water-logged potholes. Through the sleet, Senn spotted some lights in the distance, suggesting he was close to the jetty.

After a few sputters, the engine shuddered and made a horrific metallic grating noise. Senn clenched the steering, cursing and begging loudly at the flickering dashboard lights of the empty fuel tank to keep going. But after a few more spasms, the engine stalled and died.

Senn sighed heavily, inhaled the smell of burnt oil, and waited for the adrenaline rush of being stranded to pass. On a positive note, he was a few hundred meters from the jetty. All he had to do was get out and run towards it in the freezing rain.

The jetty was desolate except for a few tugs and large ferry carriers. It looked like a commercial jetty, as Senn could not spot any private boats in the area.

But more troublingly, there was no sign of Stephan's car.

A couple of white tungsten lights lit up the small promenade, and a few old, rusty, metal shutters lined the walls along the edges of the fading building. Now soaking wet, Senn walked past the unguarded barriers and searched for any signs of Stephan or his boat.

The weather had made a remarkable recovery. The rain and wind had died down, but occasional lightning streaks erupted through the clouds. Senn looked out into the inky darkness and listened for the sound of any boats in the water.

Senn's hopes soared as he heard the distinct sound of a speed boat heading out into the lagoon with all its lights turned off against all rules of maritime navigation. If this was Stephan, he was taking an immense risk of being out at sea this way.

But Senn could not see the boat or its destination in the open water. Stephan's car was also nowhere. He walked to the end of the jetty and carefully studied the metal shutters in the wall. There were three next to each other, and all padlocked shut.

Then Senn looked up and saw a small room on the level above with steps leading down to the jetty. Senn climbed the stairs and opened the door. Inside was a narrow row of hatches connecting to the rooms below. Senn tested each hatch and found two locked, but the final one yanked open to reveal a spiral staircase leading down to a parking garage. And in the darkness, Senn could make out the distinct outline of Stephan's Maserati!

He'd been here.

Senn walked to the end of the promenade and saw an empty parking spot and some fresh mud on the floor around the mooring anchors.

The unmarked boat in the ocean could only be Stephan's.

The more Senn thought about it, the more apparent it got that Stephan was trying to help protect Laura.

From the first email he sent asking for Senn's help to backing him with Colonel Taino and then telling him about Laura's ghost encounter in the Teatro.

Senn remembered the strange remark Stephan had made when they first met. Stephan had begun by saying Laura would be delighted to know Senn was in Venice looking for her. It didn't feel out of place then, but in hindsight, they were all Stephan's cryptic attempts to show Senn he was protecting Laura without explicitly saying he knew where she was.

Just then, his phone buzzed. It was Anna messaging him.

Senn, relieved to see her message, told her where he was, what he'd found, and how he needed a ride out. A few minutes later, she called him.

"Senn," Anna began in an excited voice, "I've just called the Lido police station; they're sending a car to pick you up. You're crazy to chase Stephan in the middle of a storm. But I'm sure he will come back from wherever he is, and then we can pick him up."

Senn thanked Anna and replied, "Yes, we need to talk to him. He knows where Laura is."

CHAPTER 35

THE MOLE IN TAINO'S FORCE

Senn felt dampened as he finished consoling Laura's traumatized parents on the phone, who craved good news about her whereabouts and well-being after twelve days since she had disappeared.

Senn dreaded these regular calls with Linda and Simon. Without concrete evidence of Laura, he felt like an imposter trying to spin hope out of thin air. Laura's father, Simon, was a revered sky diving instructor who'd had to retire a few years ago after a spinal cord injury during a dive that resulted in him semi-paralyzed from the waist down. Linda, Laura's mum, was a retired music professor at the Royal College of Music in London, and they lived in Esher, just outside London. Since Laura's disappearance, she'd struggled with hypertension and insomnia due to the lack of information about her only child.

Senn hoped that interrogating Stephan would shed much-needed light on Laura's location as he waited for Anna to join him before heading to Lido Island to inspect Stephan's confiscated car.

As Senn greeted her at the bright but frosty St. Marco Square, Anna looked perturbed, with her hair clumsily coiled into a loose bun and her face puffy from lack of sleep. Anna sheepishly smiled at Senn from behind her aviator Ray Bans and apologized for being late.

She looked confused and irritable as they boarded the Vaporetto to Lido Island. But before Senn could ask her about that, Anna said she'd heard from Col. Taino from his undisclosed protected location and recounted what he told her about the attempt on his life.

Anna narrated that after they left his office, the colonel got a call who claimed he had a mole in his force working with the mafia and planning to assassinate him. And then the man hung up abruptly.

The colonel said he'd received crank calls like this before, so he did not make much of this one and continued working and then went to the toilet after a few minutes. He was about to come out when a massive explosion knocked him off his feet, and he passed out for a few seconds. When he regained consciousness, he saw thick smoke creeping in from under the door and quickly filling up the bathroom. He managed to climb out of his open skylight in the bathroom and run out of the rear service balcony. Some of his officers met him and whisked him away to a safe location where he is now. His family was moved out of Venice and to a secret location as well.

"But the thing Uncle was most troubled by," said Anna, a little breathless, "was that the bomb was *30 minutes late*. According to the forensic team's assessment, the timer was faulty, so it paused or slowed down and took 30 minutes longer." Looking slightly afraid, Anna said, "We were in his office when it was *supposed* to detonate!"

Senn's eyes widened as he contemplated him and Anna as collateral damage in the colonel's assassination.

"Where was the bomb?" Senn asked, slightly bewildered.

Anna coughed as she zipped up her jacket tighter around her neck and replied, "He thinks it was in one of the unopened gifts he'd received for his birthday."

Senn nodded, recalling the desk full of presents when he placed the chocolates they'd bought for Taino. To Senn, the daring, albeit botched, attempt on Taino's life only confirmed his fear that the mole inside the police HQ was an unfazed vicious operator capable of deep infiltration and brutal tactics at the highest levels of the Venetian police.

No one was safe.

But whoever called to warn the colonel was trying to protect him, making him an ally. Senn asked Anna if the colonel had any information on the caller.

Anna looked confused and replied, “I asked him, but he avoided answering the question and said, '*He had some ideas but couldn’t say anymore.*’”

Senn felt hopeful hearing that. He sounded like he was close to solving the identity of the mystery caller. The mafia had crossed the line, and it was time to strike them back fast and decisively.

As the Vaporetto docked on Lido Island, a police officer was waiting to drive them to the jetty. On the way, the officer briefed them about the situation.

Stephan’s car was still unclaimed, and undercover police were waiting to speak to him as soon as he docked. They had intercepted a radio signal from the boat at Isola Maltesi, an uninhabited brush and camping forest area about 20 km west of Alberoni.

Anna looked puzzled as she heard this and exclaimed, “Maltesi! Why would Stephan go there? There’s nothing there.” The officer nodded in agreement and was unsure why Stephan would be there.

CHAPTER 36

SENN TAKES STOCK

Senn walked onto the St. Marco square just as the first rays of the sun hit the domes' top spires. He'd not slept for more than 24 hours. Senn liked to walk when he felt overwhelmed and needed to clear his head.

He and Anna had waited hours for Stephan to return to the jetty, but he hadn't shown up.

Senn had shared his theory with Anna about Laura and Stephan being lovers, but she seemed unconvinced. Anna thought Laura would never get involved with someone like Stephan. She guessed the bracelet was a gift from her friend Sophie which she had put inside an empty Teatro box. Her reaction weakened Senn's theory significantly, disheartening him, yet he remained open-minded.

All his probable suspects and witnesses in Laura's abduction/disappearance were either missing or murdered.

1. Luca - *Murdered.*
2. Dario - *Murdered.*

3. Mia- *Murdered.*
4. Stephan - *Missing.*
5. Laura- *Missing (for thirteen days.)*

And to poison the water further, the threat to himself and his friends was ever escalating.

1. Col. Taino, a key ally of Senn's, was now in a secret protected location after a failed attempt on his life.
2. Senn had been assaulted, stalked, and jeered at by the same man who was most likely Mia's assassin, not to mention the death threat chatter on the dark mafia websites.
3. The only person who had avoided a full-blown mafia vengeance attack so far was Anna—but even she had received death threat emails, causing the colonel to appoint her an armed escort.

As Senn looked out over the waves at San Giorgio and Lido Island further ahead, he was puzzled by the significance of Alberoni as a location.

Stephen had departed from Alberoni jetty, a few kilometers away from the warehouse and the cave. It was as if Alberoni was a gateway to a hidden location that both Stephan and Laura had dissolved into.

From what Senn could tell, Stephan was devastated by the death of his mother and ready to leave Venice. He had stopped all rehearsals for his musical scheduled for opening in three weeks, and all theatre booking sites were offering replacement shows instead. Stephan had paid off all the actors for the production in advance and closed the Teatro indefinitely in mourning Mia's death.

Senn had tried to call him a couple of times, and both times his phone had gone to voicemail, but when he called him last night, the message was different. It said the number was invalid, suggesting he had canceled his phone.

The last time Senn had seen Stephan, he was in a deep disguise, further confirming his plans to get out of Venice unrecognized.

Senn noticed a local bar was open, ordered a coffee, picked up the local newspaper, and scanned the headlines. The newspapers were still reporting on the attempt on Col. Taino's life and, to Senn's alarm, beginning to speculate his collusion in the mafia's underworld activities as a reason for the attempt on his life.

Senn did not believe that theory at all. From what he knew of the colonel, he was an honest cop trying his best to catch the bad guys and make Venice a safe and peaceful city.

The bar owner smiled at Senn as he put a steaming cup of coffee on his table. The morning sun was lighting up the square and welcoming some early tourists.

Senn flicked on through the paper and stopped at a feature story on the islands around Venice. His eyes spotted the picture of Ottagono Alberoni, one of the tourist attractions.

It was an octagonal island about 10 kms out of Venice and equidistant between Lido Island and Venice. The article described the island, built around the 1600s, as a watch tower against enemy ships. It served as a prison for political prisoners for a while before finally becoming private property. It housed an art gallery that sometimes opened to the public in the summer.

The article showed pictures of the place with its beautiful garden, marble and stone statues, and some art displayed in the gallery.

Senn's pulse quickened when he spotted someone familiar in the picture. Standing looking at one of the paintings was Mia! Senn had to clean his glasses once to ensure he was not dreaming. But it was her!

What a coincidence!

But then Senn had a blinding thought. What if Mia had something to do with the Ottagono?

Senn began googling the Ottogano, which quickly led to its listing on the local art council as one of the art galleries that occasionally opened to the public. Senn was fascinated by this discovery. He had to find out who owned the gallery.

It was almost 8.45 AM. The art council office was a few minutes from St. Marco Square and opened at 9 AM. He paid for the coffee and the newspaper, which he rolled and tucked into his jacket, and began walking towards the arts council.

All he had to know was who owned the art gallery, and he would know who owned the Ottogano.

CHAPTER 37

STOLEN FROM A PRIVATE ART GALLERY

"Courage in danger is half the battle."

—PLAUTUS

Senn stood shivering outside the locked ornate metal doors of the Art Council of Venice. It was 9.15 AM, but the bland concrete building looked deserted.

Senn double-checked for the opening time. The day was bright but bitterly cold. He grasped the morning newspaper in his pocket with the story about the Ottagono deli Alberoni and its small, private gallery. He planned to pose as a tourist and ask if he could see the gallery.

At 9.20, he saw a short, middle-aged lady wearing thick glasses and a dusty pink dress appeared from inside the building and look curiously at Senn as she unlocked the door. Senn stepped up and asked if she could help answer some of his questions about an art gallery he wanted to visit. At first, the woman looked a bit wary of Senn's question but then let him in and asked him to wait for the official opening of 9.30.

Senn nodded and apologized for being early. He needed her help, so he had no plans to challenge her on the correct opening times.

She returned a few minutes later, invited Senn into a small anteroom, sat behind a large computer screen, and then raised her eyes over her glasses and asked the gallery's name.

Senn pulled his newspaper out, showed her the picture of the Ottagono, and asked about the art gallery inside it. Senn made it sound like he was very excited to discover this place.

The woman scanned the newspaper and then typed something into her records, squinting as if she was confused at what she was reading. Her typing became a bit more vigorous as she focused harder on the screen. The lady seemed to have woken from her slumber as her eyes darted from right to left like billiard balls on a snooker table.

Finally, after satisfying herself, the lady looked at Senn and, in a sympathetic voice, said, "Sorry, sir, but the art gallery's permanently closed."

"Oh, no. When?" Senn asked, sounding disappointed.

The lady looked at her screen and paused to ensure she was reading it correctly. "Last week."

Senn, surprised, prodded her to know who shut it down and why.

She looked at her screen again, looked back at Senn, and said, "The notes here say because of a robbery."

Senn, looking bewildered, asked, "Oh no! do they say what was stolen?"

The woman, now a bit confused and frazzled, looked at Senn sheepishly and said she did not know for sure, but she could ask her supervisor if she had any more details as she was relatively new in the job.

Senn agreed to wait as he pretended to be curious to know more.

A few minutes later, an older lady entered the room, sat across from Senn, and reconfirmed that the Rossi Gallery had been permanently closed after a robbery a month ago. Senn's ears perked up when he heard the name of the gallery. Looking innocent, he asked if the gallery and Teatro Rossi were connected or just a coincidence. Both ladies smiled in unison, pleased with their knowledge, and confirmed that the gallery belonged to the same owners.

Senn had his answer!

The Rossi gallery *did* belong to Mia and Stephan and matched Stephan's recent string of shutdowns of his affairs in Venice.

But the robbery sounded suspicious.

Still looking sad and frustrated, Senn lamented to the ladies that his friend had told him to go there to see a rare Modigliani.

"I hope the Modigliani was not one of the stolen paintings," Senn said in an alarmed tone.

The women, now feeling sorry for Senn's lost opportunity, offered to check what the registered works of the gallery were, including the Modigliani, and if the gallery had declared any details of the robbery.

After some more typing and mumbling, the senior manager smiled and said, "Yes, it's this one. They had one of his signed works. And yes, unfortunately, it was reported stolen a month ago." Then she turned the monitor around so Senn could see the painting.

Senn's jaw dropped in shock.

It was the same painting of the woman in a red dress he had found stashed behind the tarpaulin in Stephan's basement. He had shut down the gallery, reported the masterpiece missing, and hidden it in the Teatro basement.

Senn admired the painting with many pained sounds of "Ooh! Oh, Wow! and What a shame!" After a few more groans, Senn said goodbye and left. The women bid him goodbye and again commiserated about his inability to see the painting.

Senn was excited as he exited the building, stood outside, adjusted to the bright sunlight, and put on his sunnys.

In the little square, shops were starting to open, and an old homeless man sat on the bench selling packets of bird feed while a flock of pigeons flew all around his head as he scattered grain and tried to keep them calm.

Senn smiled, walked up to the man, and offered to buy his bird feed. Senn pulled out some pocket change, but the coins slipped out of his fingers. Senn apologized and bent to pick it up.

Suddenly, he heard a strange, sharp, whizzing sound streak past his ear and land with a crunching sound behind him.

Senn turned and was horrified to see the shocked face of the man, and blood gushing out of his neck. An arrow had impaled through his neck and lodged into the wooded bench behind him. It all happened so fast and quietly that even the pigeons were unaware of the gory site and kept flying around the man's face, pecking at the feed from his still outstretched limp hands.

Senn instinctively knew the bolt was for him, and another one was heading for his head any second. He shouted, "Call an ambulance," to the shop owner closest to the dying man as he sprinted to the end of the square, ran into a narrow alley, and kept running as fast as possible.

He'd narrowly escaped a lethal crossbow attack in broad daylight.

CHAPTER 38

HIDE AND SEEK WITH SERIAL KILLERS

"Find out what a person fears most and that is where he will develop next."

—CARL JUNG

Senn's hands shook uncontrollably as he struggled to double-lock his apartment door. Somebody had just tried to kill him. The assassin's crossbow arrow had missed him by a whisker and sadly killed an innocent, homeless bystander.

Senn shuddered with fear as he felt like a hunted animal in freezing Venice.

Someone had followed him to his meeting at the arts council and positioned themselves at a sniper distance to get a clear view of him when he returned. It was disturbing to realize the assassin was a trained crossbow marksman with an audacious ability to strike in broad daylight in the middle of a bustling square.

The choice of weapon was intriguing. A crossbow was a silent but vicious close-range weapon in an expert's hand, readily available in Italian stores for anyone with a hunting license. Whoever had fired it on Senn knew how to kill without leaving a trace.

Senn was reasonably sure the assassin would strike again, but this time closer to his home. His stalker knew where he stayed and was either trying to kill him himself or had given his address to the killers. Senn had so far callously ignored the warnings from the police and Anna about the mafia death threats on him.

But after this morning's attack, he had to find a safer place to operate.

Senn sent a quick message to Anna, with a picture of the article and a tag: 'Look at the picture.' And telling her to call him as he checked for alternative accommodation online.

In all the panic of the attack, Senn tried to stay positive and remembered he'd made a breakthrough at the arts council about finding Stephan. He now knew Mia and Stephan owned the Ottagono. Therefore this mysterious, obscure building in the middle of the ocean (and close to Alberoni island) was an ideal hiding spot for Stephan, which he planned to investigate imminently.

The police had no time to help him search for Laura anymore as Col. Taino's safety was their prime focus, and Senn was OK with that.

He just had to keep going and find Stephan. The thought uppermost on his mind now was—*were Laura and Stephan in the Ottagono.?*

The last known location of Laura alive was in Stephan's boat moored in Lido—a few kilometers from the Ottagono. Secondly, Stephan had disappeared using the commercial jetty in Alberoni, also a few kilometers from Ottagono.

As he hurriedly finished packing, he saw Anna's message flash on his phone. She had Covid and lost her voice and had a high fever.

Senn felt terrible for her and decided not to bother her with the new developments until she felt stronger.

Senn looked at his watch. It was almost noon. He had enough time to get to the Ottagono and be back to pretend to leave for the airport.

He'd found an apartment on Airbnb, which he quickly booked for a week. He planned to go to the airport, wait there, and then return to the new apartment late at night to throw anyone off his tail.

He was almost at the door when he heard a knock. When Senn asked who it was, there was no answer. After a few seconds came another knock. Louder and more urgent.

Senn pulled his push dagger out of its holster, tightened his grip around the handle, and demanded more firmly who it was.

This time a nervous female voice answered, “Hello, I’m your neighbor. I have a package for you.”

CHAPTER 39

THE FIRES RAGE UNDER THE SMOKE

"One mark of a great soldier is that he fights on his terms or fights not at all."

—SUN TZU

Senn opened the door and saw a young woman standing outside holding a brown envelope, looking nervous. She handed the package to him and said, "The courier left it by mistake at my apartment. It was for Laura. I know you're her friend, so I thought you should have it, and maybe it helps to find her."

Senn had met all the neighbors, so he was curious about this woman. When asked, she told him she was the daughter of one of the elderly residents and had been out of town for a few weeks.

The woman turned to leave, and Senn stopped her and asked if she'd seen or heard anything suspicious while still in the building.

The woman furrowed her brow and replied, "Not really. She was a late-nighter. I used to hear her moving around 'til quite late. She lives above my flat, and I'm a light sleeper as I need to help my mum with the toilet."

She continued, "Laura normally returned to the room around midnight after rehearsals. But sometimes she returned home with someone. A man."

Senn's eyes widened. "With a man? Are you sure? Did you ever see him?"

The woman shook her head. "No, but I could hear them talking. I could not hear their words, but I remember his deep and heavy voice."

"When did you last hear Laura with the man?" Senn asked, trying to zero in on the date.

"I think it was the 3rd of Feb," she replied tentatively. And then she added with much more certainty, "I'm sure. I left for Poland on the 5th."

"And did you hear anything else that time?" Senn asked, desperate for more information, knowing it was the last night before she disappeared.

The woman shook her head. "No, they left together. It was almost one in the morning. I was still studying and remember wondering where Laura was going so late again."

Senn asked, "Did you think Laura was in danger?"

The woman's nervousness returned as she shook her head and hands as if to claim innocence and said in a high-pitched voice, "No, no, not at all, sir. I thought she knew this man well as I remember them laughing with each other as they walked past my room. She sounded fine."

"Why didn't you tell this to the police?"

She looked a bit sheepish and answered, "I just got back from Poland, and the landlord told me about Laura and said you were her friend, so I'm telling you now. I am also fine to tell the police if you want me to."

Senn could tell the woman was telling the truth and did not know much more than what she'd told him. He wondered if Laura had left that night with a man; she knew him well enough to let him into her room. But why did Laura come back with this man and then leave again? What was the reason for her returning? It was a pity that the house did not have CCTV; otherwise, he could have seen him.

Senn looked at the woman and smiled. "No, I think it's fine. I'll let them know, and they may want to talk to you, and they'll get in touch."

She looked relieved at Senn's reaction, relaxed a bit, then at the brown Amazon packet, and said, "I hope this package gives some clues to where she is. She is a lovely person, always smiling and kind. I hope she's safe and well, and I hope you find her soon."

Senn nodded, said goodbye, and closed the door.

Senn looked at the package with excitement. Now he had conclusive evidence that Laura met a man at her place the night she vanished. It could be Stephan.

He stared at the small box, placed it on the table, and got a butter knife to cut the tape. The package was not heavy and did not rattle inside either. Senn carefully opened the lid and pulled out an expensive-looking, blue-striped silk scarf. It looked like something Stephan wore, except his were mainly dull black. The clues were piling up that linked Laura closely to a man she trusted, including a male gift that looked like something Stephan wore.

Was this man Stephan!? Senn was desperate to find out.

He was late as he stepped out of the flat and walked towards the canal for the waiting water taxi to the airport. Senn dearly hoped his visit to the Ottagono would unveil their hiding place.

He planned to go to the airport, leave the bags in an airport locker and then rent a private boat to take him to the Ottagono by sunset. This way, he hoped to get rid of the tail, which could be following him.

Senn got in the taxi and watched the slanting sun skid off the wake of the shimmering water as they left the grand city behind. Senn was nervous but hopeful that the Ottagono held vital clues to Stephan and Laura's location.

At the airport, Senn walked up to the information desk, located the locker service company, put his and Laura's suitcase into the rented box, and locked it.

Then he entered the public toilets and locked himself in one of the cubicles.

He removed a baseball cap from his backpack with an attached shoulder-length, curly hair wig. He pulled a black windcheater over his winter jacket and put on his covid mask and sizeable black frame glasses to complete the overhaul. He laughed when he saw his new look. He looked far more suspicious than his usual self.

He stepped out of the toilet and scanned the area. A few nuns were looking at the departure screens trying to locate their flights, and a few families were sleeping in chairs in the rear of the hall. Besides these people, Senn did not spot anyone who could be a potential tail.

He walked past some police officers and airport staff, exited the departure lounge, and turned towards the water taxi point.

He walked to the far end of the jetty and spotted the tiny, white dinghy bobbing on the water. A short, grey-bearded bald man came out of the boat and greeted Senn with a smile. Senn smiled back and said, "Hello, captain. Thank you for meeting me at short notice. Col. Taino had said I could call you if I needed some last-minute help."

The captain smiled back. "My pleasure, Mr. Senn. I am happy to help a friend of Col. Taino. Ottagono is about thirty minutes from here. But we better hurry before the weather gets worse."

Senn jumped in and stood next to the captain as he expertly maneuvered the boat into the open water, heading to the private island of Ottagono at the horizon's edge.

CHAPTER 40

THE BROODING OTTAGONO

"Skinny guys fight 'til they're burger."

—CHUCK PALAHNIUK

Angry storm clouds thundered menacingly over the dot of a boat as Senn and the captain spotted *Ottagono* in the bleak distance.

The octagonal, red brick walls rose out of the agitated ocean like a drowning skyscraper with just its top floors visible. Shooting out of the twenty-meter-high walls was a wild herd of trees whose tentacular branches buffeted the raging winds.

The Ottagono was one of three 18th-century brick-and-stone engineering feats built by the Venetians as defensive watch towers in the lagoon against the invasions of the Ottoman empire. They had mostly been forgotten in the 19th century but revived in utility as torture islands and prisons in the Second World War and then swiftly sold off to wealthy Venetian families like Mia's after the war.

Senn's numb fingers clasped the freezing metal rod of the boat tighter as he looked in awe and trepidation at the looming monolith, which grew larger and larger as they approached it while waves battered it from all sides.

The light dimmed as they reached the southern end of the Ottagono. Unable to find an entrance, the captain followed the curve of the building, and just as they turned the corner, Senn spotted a bright blue water scooter bobbing outside an open, rugged wooden door.

Senn's hopes soared. Someone was inside. Maybe it was Stephan. And Laura was with him.

Safe.

The captain maneuvered the boat parallel to the sodden door and helped Senn get his foot on the metal steps that jutted out of the wall. It looked like the service door to the island, and a giant Wisteria had spread its branches across it, making the entrance treacherous. The captain looked at his watch, told Senn he had about an hour to check out the place, and offered to wait until he returned.

Senn nodded and cautiously entered the dark, forgotten, forested Ottagono island.

From the corner of his eyes, he saw a snake's inky tail slither into the bush just as the wings of a startled bird flapped somewhere in the trees above. Eerie hissing sounds came from all around, most probably caused by the wind rushing through the thick foliage. The ground was flooded with ankle-deep water, and from the swirls, he could tell it was deeper up ahead.

Senn instantly felt unsure and unwelcome.

A narrow trail that disappeared into the dense undergrowth was the only viable path Senn could see. Anxious yet compelled, Senn waded into the vortex.

After a few feet of walking, as expected, the path dipped, and soon he was in waist-deep water that coiled around him, caking his clothes with mud and slimy moss. The high tide had backed into the island, mixed with the rain, and flooded all the low-lying areas. The smell of rotting flesh momentarily overwhelmed his senses as the carcass of a bloated seagull floated past him in the water.

After a few minutes of wading through the leech-infested water, the bush cleared, and an outline of a white house appeared in the distance.

The water level receded as Senn emerged from the undergrowth and got a clear view of the structure for the first time. He had arrived at the rear of a long shed resembling a Second World War barrack. It was a simple brick structure with three-meter-high walls and a row of small, barred windows stretched across the entire building. The building was at least 200 meters long, and Senn reckoned it had been constructed during the war as living quarters for soldiers and later repaired and repainted for use as a gallery by Mia and Stephan.

It was a well-preserved building compared to the surrounding wilderness, but the windows were all boarded, with no sign of life inside.

Senn looked for an entrance as he stealthily walked along the wall while watching for any human activity. As Senn approached the building corner, he tensed when he heard shuffling footsteps on the far end. Senn pinned himself to the wall and listened intently.

The person was moving something heavy along the concrete floor, which made a sharp, screeching sound as it moved. After a few seconds, it stopped. Then the dragging continued, this time accompanied by a faint, melodic whistle.

Senn could tell it was a man by the intermingling of his whistles with humming some broken words of an Italian song as he walked around again, dragging things on the floor. It sounded like the man was comfortable in the place and knew what he was doing. It did not sound like Stephan, but Senn was not sure. Was the estate caretaker on his regular site visit?

The man continued whistling while moving inside, suggesting there was a side entrance.

The wind changed direction and suddenly brought a distinct smell of cigarillos.

Senn knew that dreaded tobacco.

The thought triggered panic in Senn's mind. He had to get a better vantage point to be sure.

He noticed that a few meters from the main building was a small garage/tool shed-like structure. Senn reckoned if he could sprint across to that building without being spotted, he would stay hidden but directly see the door and who the man was. The whistling continued, still coming from inside, accompanied by the same pulling of heavy objects across the floor.

It was now or never. Senn hurled himself out of his spot and sprinted as silently as possible until he reached the opposite brick wall. His heart raced as he froze and listened, hoping the man had not spotted him.

The whistling and the dragging stopped abruptly.

Senn, who by now was well hidden, peeked out as he heard footsteps approaching the door.

Senn's jaw dropped, and a shiver ripped through his spine when he saw the man who emerged with a suspicious frown on his face—his ruthless stalker.

CHAPTER 41

PRYING OPEN A VENOMOUS JAW

From his new hideout, Senn glared with contempt at his stalker.

Part of him wanted to step out and flog him for all his intimidatory behavior over the past days. But he preferred to wait and find out what the man was up to on the island before confronting him. He was dealing with a hellish man capable of extreme violence, and additionally, Senn was sure the man's antennas were already up by the sounds of his movements. Had he followed him and schemed a welcome trap?

Senn watched as the wiry, lean man hunched at the covered portico entrance, wearing an oversized open leather jacket and embroidered cowboy boots. His chest was exposed and covered in tattoos. He stood there smoking a cigarillo and scoured the bush through slitted, hooded eyes. After a few seconds of indecision, the man began humming again and turned to re-enter the house but jerked around with a vicious, manic look and strode straight in Senn's direction.

Senn braced himself for a face-off. He gripped his push dagger at his ankle, ready to strike. The crowded bush was disadvantageous for Senn to confront the man, but he had no choice. Senn held his breath, unclipped the dagger from the holster, and waited for him to turn the corner.

But just a second before Senn could strike, the man stopped in his tracks, spewed out a loud, disgusted grunt, and repeatedly cursed at something. Seconds later, Senn saw a giant rodent (almost the size of a small pig) race past him into the undergrowth. Senn almost gasped in shock at the animal's size and foot-long tail, barely managing to keep silent.

The man halted just a few feet from Senn and continued to cuss the beaver. Senn's heart raced as the tip of the man's boots poked out from behind the wall. After a few seconds, he turned and walked back into the house, probably satisfied that he'd solved the mystery noise he'd heard.

Senn relaxed the grip on his dagger and let out a sigh, but in his mind, he kicked himself for not pouncing on the man just then. The beaver had startled the man and left him vulnerable to being attacked and subdued by Senn. But he'd hesitated, and now it was too late for regrets.

The man had dragged a heavy, battered metal table into the porch and placed it in front of the door like a blockade.

A large twenty-liter, military green canister sat on the table, along with some rope and large, black plastic bags.

It all looked alarmingly sinister. Senn dreaded thinking about the man's motives; what he was constructing looked like material for torching body bags. There was no sign of Stephan and Laura.

It was getting dark, and Senn was running out of time.

He wasn't sure if his ride would wait for him too long after the agreed time or if he would come to his rescue if he needed help, even though he was Col. Taino's contact.

The door had long, indigo velvet curtains billowing out from the sides. He reckoned if he snuck into the building unnoticed, he could temporarily hide behind them and plan his next step.

Not hearing any sounds, Senn dashed towards the door when a woman's chilling scream rang out from the far corner of the dark house and reverberated through the building, sending shock waves down his spine.

A churlish giggle and laugh followed the scream.

Senn, sensing it was now or never, ran down the narrow, dark hall, reached the door where the sounds were coming from, and kicked it hard, making it fly open with a loud cracking noise.

His worst nightmare confronted him.

He saw a terrified Laura *and* Stephan with their hands tied behind their backs, lying in a bed facing each other while the man leaned over them, sniggering with an oversized jagged-edged hunting knife inches from Laura's face.

Senn lunged at the man with both hands to try and dislodge his grip on his enormous, steel blade. The man, caught unawares for a second, felt the full force of Senn's body on him as they both lost their balance and fell to the floor.

Senn pinned the man's head down as he tried to get his hands on the knife that had fallen a few feet from them. The man, shocked at the sudden attack, tried to regain control by boxing Senn's face with his left hand as his right reached out to regain control of the knife. But his fingers missed the handle, and it slid under the bed.

Senn took the blow directly on his left eye and felt a gash open instantly, blood spurting out and blurring his vision. The man was wearing knuckle armor.

Senn managed to duck his head into the man's armpit to avoid the next blow as he grabbed his throat and squeezed with all his strength.

Suddenly, the man started to make a bizarre, howling noise. He let Senn choke him for a few seconds as if enjoying the pressure on his neck. It was almost like he had become possessed. He kicked Senn repeatedly in the stomach with his knees while making that sick, howling noise as he freed Senn's hands off his throat. Senn could feel the man had magically amassed superhuman strength despite his wiry bony frame.

Senn pulled out his ankle push-dagger and slashed at the man's face. The man noticed the blade and blocked him with his elbow, which dislodged it out of Senn's palm and landed on the bed beside a horrified Laura and Stephan.

The cut over Senn's eyes was gushing blood and blurring his vision. The man lunged at Senn and, this time, head-butted him in the same wound, making Senn scream out with pain and try to evade the next blow. Senn picked up a chair and threw it at him while darting behind a pillar in the room to get some distance.

The man stopped howling, stared at Senn with a feigned look of frustration, and said, "What took you so long, darling!?"

Then he pulled out a Glock 17 from his hip, aimed at Senn, and pulled the trigger.

CHAPTER 42

DEADLY CLOSE WITH THE DEVIL

Senn felt an excruciating burning sensation as the bullet grazed his ear and shattered the window behind him. Caught off-guard, Senn uttered a loud groan and dashed out of the room into the dark corridor as another shot whizzed past his shoulder as he exited the door.

The man was aiming straight at his head!

Senn had to decide which way to go. He could run out and get help or stay close to Laura. Senn sprinted into the dark, cold house, frantically turning all the door handles to see if anyone would offer a sanctuary to hide.

The house was enormous, with rows of doors on either side of the cavernous hallway, which abruptly bifurcated with one corridor turning a sharp left and descending six feet to a lower ground floor. He ran down the steps and tried the first door handle.

Locked.

Next.

Locked.

Senn, now desperate, reached the last door, turned the handle, and kicked the door.

It opened!

Senn rushed in and desperately looked for a bolt to lock the door but found none.

His lungs were screaming for air, and he was bleeding profusely from the cut over his eye and ear. Senn tried to steady his nerves as he listened intently to the man's footsteps.

He could distinctly hear the man walking closer and closer to where he was.

Senn, in that instant, realized he had to overpower the man.

He couldn't keep hiding anymore. The darkness was his best bet to try and lure him into the room and subdue him, dead or alive. He still had a concealed push dagger but wished he had something more significant to strike the man down.

Senn adjusted his eyes to the darkness and scanned the room's contents. The place was an old pantry with an enormous chimney behind him with large, heavy metal pots on the shelves next to it. Apart from this, the area was barren.

But he glimpsed a metal stoker leaning inside the chimney. The wrought iron rod was about four feet tall and had a couple of metal hooks.

He stretched his arms out, carefully lifted the heavy stoker without disturbing the other implements, wrapped his hand around it, and waited behind the door, ready to pounce when the man entered or passed by.

The man had reached the top of the steps and stopped.

The silence was tantalizing as both men tried to sense where the other was and read each other's minds and moves. Senn tightened his grip on the rod as he heard the man start to come down the steps toward the slightly ajar door.

Just as the man entered the room, the eerie hoot of an owl shattered the silence startling the man. Senn, unperturbed, let out a gut-wrenching scream and struck the man's outstretched arm holding the gun with all his might.

With a resounding clang, the gun slipped out of the man's hands and skidded to the center of the room.

The man screamed in pain as Senn pounced on him and struck him again with the rod across his face. The man moaned as he tried to pull the rod out of Senn's grasp and growled.

A deep gash had cut the man's lips, and blood was oozing. One of his eyes was swollen and bleeding. Even in the darkness, Senn could see the man's bloodshot eyes staring at him as they fought to control the metal rod.

The man suddenly released the rod and dived onto the floor to grab the gun. Senn anticipated the move and pounced on him, pinning him and locking his arms around his throat while wrapping his legs like a snake and tightening his grip.

The man's wrist was badly broken as his right hand was bent out of shape and hanging free from the arm. Senn used all his might to tighten his choke hold as the man fought hard to loosen it.

The gun lay a few feet away as the men wrestled each other. The man's resistance started weakening as his body grew limp, and he started to black out.

But in a sudden surge of energy, the man somehow pulled a knife out of his left boot and stabbed Senn repeatedly in the leg.

Senn let out a blood-curdling scream. The severity of the pain made Senn release the choke hold and focus on blocking the knife. Seeing Senn weaken his grip, the man lunged towards the gun again and managed to grab it despite his broken wrist. He turned and pointed it at Senn's face, bared his stained teeth in a deathly smile, and rasped, "Bye-bye, Bluebird," and pulled the trigger.

But the gun jammed.

The man looked confused at the gun and then back at Senn. Senn, who had his hands on his dagger under his belt, pulled it out and stabbed the man straight into his neck.

With the last ounce of strength left in him, Senn wrapped his blood-soaked legs around the man and, with both hands, shifted all his weight onto the three-inch blade and held it down as he watched the man gag for breath and then slowly enter shock and eventually stop struggling.

CHAPTER 43

THE MAYHEM'S CONTRAIL

An exhausted Senn prostrated over the man's blood-soaked, lifeless body, with his hands maintaining the pressure on the dagger lodged deep into his lacerated throat.

Senn shivered with adrenaline as he pulled out the blade, rolled over, panting, and leaned on the chimney wall to reclaim his senses while the dead man's lifeless grey eyes stared blankly back at him from the floor.

Senn winced at the multiple bloody gashes glaring out of his torn jeans, and his hands and arms soaked in blood.

It didn't feel like he'd fought a man, more like a rabid beast who refused to surrender and kept resurging in a gorier form every time Senn thought he'd capitulated.

Senn recognized the familiar signs of the double-winged tattoo on the man's palm, confirming that his hunter had stalked him since his arrival in Venice.

Senn shut his eyes and clenched his fist in gratitude for being still alive.

He crawled on all fours, patted the man's clothes for ID, and found his wallet, which he shoved into his pocket to examine later. He also removed the gun, still hooked to the man's fingers, and checked for safety before putting it into his pocket.

Senn propped himself up using the stoker and hobbled towards the room where he'd left Laura and Stephan. His prime worry was that the psychopath might have hurt them before coming after him.

Senn winced in pain with every dragging step he took in the dark corridor when he heard a shuffle of hastening steps approaching the building from outside.

Senn froze, unsure of who it was, leaned back into the crevasse of one of the doors, and waited. Senn knew he was toast if this was the dead guy's friend.

An intense beam of light shone into the hallway, followed by a shout, "This is the police. Come out with your hands above your head," that reverberated down the hallway.

Senn stepped into the light with his hands raised and shouted, "Don't shoot. I am coming out."

Senn hobbled a few steps with his hands raised but lost his balance and crumpled on the ground. A burly man in a black leather jacket rushed forward and grabbed

Senn. The man's eyes filled with worry when he saw all the blood on Senn's hands and body.

Senn kept his hands above his head and said, "You need to help my friends in that room behind you." The officer nodded as another few plain-clothed men and women entered the corridor with their firearms pointing at Senn.

The last person to enter the house was the scared-looking captain of the boat. He ran up to Senn, sat next to him with a shocked expression. "Oh my God, Mr. Senn, what happened to you? Are you OK?"

Senn nodded as he struggled to stay conscious as the adrenaline and blood drained out of him.

The captain continued, "I was waiting for you when I heard a woman's scream, and then I heard some gunshots. I got scared. So I called Col. Taino. He sent these guys".

Senn relaxed a bit but dreaded what the officers had found in the room where Laura and Stephan were. He hoped and prayed Laura was safe and unhurt.

Just then, one of the officers came out, holding a stack of cut tapes and ropes. He looked at Senn and said, "There's no one inside. Who was in there?"

Senn, stunned, replied, "There were two people, Laura Simmonds and Stephan Conti."

Damn! They'd escaped! Senn reckoned they'd used the knife he'd dropped while grappling with the man to saw through their handcuffs. But how did they get out? Could they still be on the island?

The officer, unsure of what he'd heard, repeated the question and, with a concerned voice, added, "The ambulance is on its way. You seem to be bleeding a lot, sir."

Senn sighed. "No, only some of it is mine." Senn pointed at the room at the end of the corridor. Senn took out the gun and the man's wallet, handed them over to the officers, and fell unconscious, exhausted.

CHAPTER 44

THE CURIOUS COVER UP

Senn propped himself up in the hospital bed to ease the pressure on his bandaged face and leg as nurses and doctors scurried around him. A couple of plain-clothed police stood guard at the door, carefully checking everyone coming in and out. Given the circumstances, he didn't mind the police protection one bit.

A short, overweight man entered and introduced himself as Pablo, a secret service officer handling the case.

In a deadpan voice, the officer looked at Senn and said, "Col. Taino sends his regards and thanks you for your bravery, Mr. Senn."

He opened his bag, pulled out a file, and said, "We also want to thank you for killing one of the most wanted mafia men in Venice, Antonio Picci, the Prince of Cocaine and one of the most dangerous and elusive drug lords in Italy."

Pablo continued, updating Senn on Antonio's operations.

Antonio ran a laundry services contract with international cruise liners. But it was a cover for his cocaine trafficking. He mixed the drugs with commercial detergent packets, making it easy for select mafia-employed men on the ships to offload the drugs at different ports where the cruise liner docked.

The officer confirmed Senn's hunch that Luca and Dario worked for Antonio and ran the drugs from the Teatro to the Lido warehouse, where Antonio received them.

Fronting as tourist boat captains, Luca and Dario rented Stephan's city taxi to hide small quantities of cocaine and transport the drugs out of the Teatro basement to Antonio.

Dario would receive the drugs from Luca on Lido Island and store them in his gym warehouse, with its secret underground access to the ocean. Antonio would then show up in the warehouse cave, pick up the drugs, and move them into passing cruise ships that regularly docked on the island.

The officer confirmed that Antonio's DNA matched the unidentified DNA found on Dario, Luca, and Mia, proving he was their assassin.

Just as the officer was leaving, Senn's phone lit up.

It was Anna.

Senn was surprised but glad she'd called him even though she was still deep in the throes of Covid and had not spoken to him for a couple of days. She sounded worried, breathless, and unusually emotional.

Anna began in a low, husky voice, "Senn! I've been so worried about you! Where the hell are you? The last I heard from you was two days ago! Two fucking days ago! You could have messaged me to say you're OK! I'm just sick in bed, not dead, you know! Damn it, Senn! I hate you when you disappear and don't tell me anything."

Senn smiled sheepishly, feeling guilty, and tried to calm her and reassure her that he was OK. She wanted to know everything that transpired on the island, so Senn brought her up to speed while sparing the gory details.

Senn finished talking and could feel a complete change of tone from Anna. Just a long pause of stunned silence. Senn had to prod her to speak, to which she exclaimed, "But you know the press is saying something completely different."

Senn, confused, replied, "I've not seen anything. What are they saying?"

Anna replied in a hissing voice, "The police have just released a statement that says an inter-mafia rivalry has broken out among different Venetian drug cartels. They are reporting similar incidents around the country. But no mention of Antonio yet."

Senn was taken aback by this news.

Anna continued, "Senn, I think the police are using Antonio's death as a trigger to carry out fake operations and kill well-known gang leaders around the country as revenge for attempting to kill Col. Taino."

"Are you sure?" Senn asked, not entirely sure about Anna's theory.

"I'm certain. Three mafia cartel leaders have died across Italy in the last 48 hours. The police are making it look like inter-gang rivalry but carrying out these operations themselves, undercover."

CHAPTER 45

THE PHONE CALL

Anna's frantic phone call had left Senn confused. Her conviction that the police were killing mafia drug lords as revenge for the attempt on Col. Taino's life was unsettling.

Col. Taino would never approve of that. He was a straight-shooting cop who did things by the book. Revenge was not his style. In any case, Senn had asked to speak to the colonel directly to regain his support for finding Laura.

The cold, salty, winter morning air carried a lingering smell of rotting fish and exhaust from the passing cruise liner past his hospital balcony. Knowing Laura was with Stephan doubled his anxiety.

Stephan was an entrenched mafia collaborator, however reluctant or disgusting it might make him feel. On the other hand, Laura was the innocent, young girl blinded by her love for Stephan, risking her life by being with him.

The longer she stayed with him, the more she was at risk of getting harmed in the crossfire between the mafia and the police. Senn kicked himself for not rushing back to find the couple on the island before they escaped. He was desperate to persuade her and Stephan to surrender to the police and come under their witness protection program.

But Senn knew Stephan didn't trust the police. He knew something sinister about the corruption in the police force, which prevented him from staying back on the island and asking for their help. And now he was on the run from the mafia and the police. And poor Laura was stuck choosing between her love and her safety. Senn could feel her colossal dilemma.

Senn's phone lit up. It was an unnamed caller. Curious, Senn picked up the call.

"Pronto," began Senn.

A deep male voice replied (Senn instantly recognized it as Stephan), "Mr. Senn, I can't stay on the phone long. But I wanted to thank you for saving Laura and my life at the Ottagono. I will pass the phone on to Laura. Please wait."

Before Senn could react, he heard the halting voice of Laura for the first time.

"Nico?" she asked cautiously.

"Yes, Laura, it's me. Are you OK?" Senn exclaimed, unable to hide his relief and delight at hearing her voice.

Laura's high-pitched voice erupted.

"I'm OK, Nico. I'm OK. Look, I can't talk long, but please tell my parents I am OK. Tell them not to worry, tell them I'm sorry. And thank you, Nico, for saving our lives. Thank you! And, Nico, you need to know this." Laura paused, drew her breath in, and said, "Stephan and I are married. I can't say more now, but you need to help him. I have to go now. Look after yourself."

And abruptly, Laura passed the phone back to Stephan.

"Mr. Senn?" Stephan was back on the line.

"Yes, I'm here," Senn replied, floored by the news that Laura was married to Stephan.

"I will be in touch again soon, but please don't tell the police anything. We need your help. Sorry, must disconnect now."

And then the call ended.

Senn looked around, suspicious of being overheard but let out a sigh, seeing the hospital breakfast staff had cleared out of the balcony.

What the hell had he just heard? Laura was married to Stephan! When did that happen? Senn's head spun at the revelation.

Senn could feel a sea change of heart coming over him for Stephan. From a man threatening Laura, he was now her loving husband, making Senn torn between separating them or helping them.

Helping Stephan also meant Senn was putting himself on the wrong side of the law.

If only he could speak to Col. Taino, he could confide in him and ask for his help to find a safe house for the couple. But he needed to wait to speak to Stephan and Laura first.

Senn's phone lit up with a message with a location pin link. Senn clicked, and it opened at the Basilica di Santa Maria Della Salute entrance on mainland Venice. Another message flashed in quick succession.

6 Am. Tomorrow. Come Alone.

It was almost 11 in the morning, and Senn was leaving the hospital in an hour. The police escorts were not far from him, and they watched Senn suspiciously from a distance, curious at the phone calls he'd been receiving.

Senn was almost sure that, given the circumstances, they were tapping his phone and knew he had spoken to Stephan and Laura. Choosing to help Laura and Stephan was crossing the line of the law. Senn juggled the white-hot options in his mind.

The police guards were a constant companion now. If he were going to meet Stephan, he had to elude the guards somehow. But that meant he was opening himself and potentially Stephan and Laura to great danger.

As he weighed his options, a nurse walked up to Senn, smiled, and said, "Mr. Senn, the hospital director would like to see you before you leave. I've arranged it so you can meet him on your way out."

Senn was slightly surprised but continued to his room for the final dressing change. Senn was heading to his new Airbnb flat that he'd booked before leaving for Ottagono.

Senn checked himself for the last time in the mirror. The right eye and ear were freshly bandaged but disguised well under his long, curly-haired wig, and baseball cap and the jeans concealed the left leg bandages quite well too.

He didn't look too bad for a guy back from the grave.

Senn walked down the long, sterile, neon-lit aisle escorted by the guards and the nurses and, at the end of the corridor, entered the office of the hospital director. No sooner had the door shut behind him than he heard a booming greeting of someone he'd dearly missed.

Col. Taino was in the house.

CHAPTER 46

THE VEILED THREAT

A beaming Col. Taino strode toward Senn and hugged him like he was welcoming back a long-lost friend. Senn was delighted, too, as they embraced and sized up each other. So much had happened to them in the last few weeks. It felt like they were meeting after years.

Senn immediately spotted a few facial changes. The colonel now had a handsome salt-and-pepper beard and a black eye patch over his right eye. A section of his forehead and scalp over his patched eye bore a distinct burn scar, a living reminder of the assassination attempt he'd survived.

He shook his hands vigorously and refused to let go of them as he led him to the couch at the far end of the room, away from the windows. Senn spotted a few armed plain-clothed men sitting in the distance, keeping a stern eye on Senn.

"Ha! Your face looks much worse than mine," the colonel jabbed at Senn in a cheery tone while his eyes studied him with kind compassion.

Senn laughed in acknowledgment. "But you're not too bad yourself."

The colonel exploded into a loud, uncontrollable belly laugh as they both enjoyed each other's dark banter. He showed him a few scars from the bomb. He'd lost his right eye due to severe burns from the shrapnel lodged in his face. The burn scars were still healing but might take months to disappear. But besides that, he was still the larger-than-life, cheerful man Senn knew and liked.

Senn updated him on his deadly encounter with Antonio and how close to a death call it was for him. The colonel nodded and listened intently as Senn described the incredible turn of events of not just discovering Laura with Stephan but that they were also married, as he'd just found out!

The colonel's eyes lit up with this new information, and he smiled. "Stephan always leaves me dumbfounded. Just when I think I've figured him out, he turns a page and amazes me. I've read him quite wrong, you know," he said, turning serious for the first time in the conversation.

"But he needs to come to us now, Senn. We can protect him and Laura only if he comes in and surrenders. We can put him and Laura into a witness protection program to keep them safe. But right now, they are both in grave danger!"

Senn, looking worried, replied, "Yes, I agree, colonel, but Stephan swears that there are rats in your police force who will betray them."

The colonel clenched his jaw and nodded. "He's not wrong, Senn. We have snakes in our force aiding the mafia, but we're looking for them. We're trying to smoke them out, but I need more time. But time is something Stephan does not have."

Turning concerned, the colonel leaned forward and whispered, "There's a 1-million-euro prize for his head on a spike. And the dark web is buzzing with interest. The word on the street is that Stephan killed Antonio and escaped with Laura. No one in the mafia knows you killed him."

Senn panicked as he imagined the escalated danger that Antonio's death had put on Laura's life.

Taino paused, drew a deep breath, and continued, "I have a team of men I trust. They will take care of Stephan and Laura. That's my promise to him and you. But you *have* to believe me." With a grim look, the colonel Stood. "If you care for Laura's life, you have to convince Stephan to come in, Senn."

Senn looking perplexed, asked, "And what if he refuses? How do we help them, then? I've just found Laura; I can't lose her."

The colonel lowered his eyes and then, through slits, looked at Senn and said, "You could ask Laura to come in. Leave Stephan and save herself. We'll find her a safe house. But they're running out of time."

Senn nodded, recognizing the grimness and the gravity of the available options.

As the colonel got ready to leave, Senn asked, " Can you clarify something for me?"

"Shoot, soldier," the colonel replied, looking curious.

"Are you killing the mafia leaders under the pretext of mock encounters?"

The colonel's eyes widened, and he looked confused for a moment at the sudden bluntness of the question and then asked, "Who told you that?"

"Anna," Senn answered in an honest tone.

The colonel stared blankly at Senn, then muttered something under his breath and replied with a pained expression, "Nonsense. Tell my niece to stop believing rumors."

The colonel motioned to his men, who stood, pulled out semi-automatic guns from below the table, and got ready to escort him out of the room.

He shook Senn's hand and, with a wry smile, said, "I don't shoot anyone in the back. Not even the devil."

Senn smiled back and shook the colonel's hand and promised to talk to Stephan and try to convince him.

The colonel gave Senn a gentle bow. "You, my friend, have come a long way. I feared the pressure might get to you, but you're getting brighter." He paused and smiled. "I'll do my best to keep you safe. But you need to do your bit. OK?"

"I'll do my best," replied Senn, waving goodbye and watching the colonel disappear through the room's back door surrounded by more than six bodyguards.

Senn leaned back in his chair and drew a heavy sigh.

He had a massive task ahead of him.

To convince Laura and Stephan to surrender to Col. Taino even though the colonel himself confessed that he was hunting a mole in his inner circle.

Was he going to make their lives better or put them in more serious (and this time) fatal danger?

Senn had a night to decide.

Was he going to see Stephan accompanied by the police or follow Stephan's strict instructions and go alone?

CHAPTER 47

MILEPOSTS IN THE DARK

Senn jolted out of bed in a sweat. He'd had that dream again, sinking helplessly into a dark, freezing ocean, unable to move a muscle. He'd started having this dream on and off since he arrived in Venice searching for Laura.

Irritated by the dream's repeated ferocity, Senn got out of his (way too soft) bed and looked at the digital clock on the wall.

4.44 AM.

From his window, he could hear the lapping sounds of the canal water a few meters away. He'd moved into his new Airbnb attic flat in Guidecca, the island immediately south of the central islands of Venice. The police escorts had booked a room in the same guest house and took turns guarding his front door.

He had to meet Stephan at 6 AM at Basilica Santa Maria della Salute on the main island and a short boat ride across the central canal.

After many deliberations, Senn had decided to meet him without his guards in tow. In case any of them were mafia moles. Senn did not want to risk their lives in any way. Especially now that Laura was always with him, he had to follow Stephan's instructions and meet him alone.

The only problem was the police guards. Before they got suspicious, he had to circumvent them and return to the flat.

Senn had hatched a *hazy* plan before going to bed and intended to try it out. The probability of it succeeding depended heavily on how quiet he could be during the exit from the building.

Senn kept the lights off and got dressed while checking the combat boots and the push daggers were in place. He pulled Laura's old faithful backpack under his jacket with her key and bracelet safely inside. He tiptoed into the toilet and glanced at his dark outline in the mirror. His all-black attire made for an ideal camouflage, including the hooded jacket that amply veiled his face's white bandages.

Senn stepped onto the covered toilet seat, looked up, and quietly unlatched the narrow skylight above.

Senn hoped it would be wide enough to let his body through. Senn pulled himself through the opening with both hands until his head and shoulders went onto the roof. The rest of his body followed quickly, and in a few seconds, Senn was crouching on the wet tiles of the building.

He planned to jump across the narrow back street onto the house, walk along the roof's edge, and descend onto the pier on the opposite side with the help of his climbing rope wrapped around his waist.

Senn listened for any movements from outside his flat and heard nothing. He looked down at the dark street about five meters below and saw it was empty. It was a typical back street in Venice, with the distance between the two houses being about a meter, an easy leap across. He checked his watch.

It was 4.57 AM. He had to wait three minutes.

At 5 AM, the church bell began to chime. The sound was gentle but resounding, loud enough to help Senn muffle his drop. The opposite house was a few feet lower than his building and had a small balcony in the attic.

Senn waited for the third chime and leapt. He landed firmly on both his feet but felt a shooting pain in his injured left leg, making him let out a reflexive grunt. He bit his lips and waited to see if he'd caused too much commotion on either side of the street.

A dog growled in the house next door, but no lights came on, and no one screamed or raised any alarm.

Senn was clear. So far, so good.

Senn, balanced on all fours, walked along the sloping roof towards the front of the house facing the canal, untied the climbing rope from his waist, and tied one end around the stack of chimneys. Then he slowly rappelled down the side of the brick wall until he reached the empty alley below.

His plan got a bit fuzzy from here onwards.

The only way to the Basilica was by ferry across the kilometer-wide canal. He checked his watch. The time now was 5.20 AM. Stephan's time request of an unearthly 6 AM was not ideal. There were no ferry services in Venice between 5 and 6 AM. Was this a trap?

On a hunch, he found Stephan's contact on his phone and shared his current location. Even though it was risky for him, Senn hoped Stephan would know where he was and try to make contact.

As he waited and pondered his next move, his phone lit up, and a message read, '*Wait there.*'

With trepidation, Senn stepped onto the deserted pier and looked out into the choppy, unchartered waters. After a few freezing minutes, he spotted the outline of a boat appearing from out of the dark fog.

It was Stephan's!

In the darkness, Senn saw the door of the cabin open, and Stephan stepped out, gave Senn a big smile, motioned him to come on board, and then went back inside. Senn could make out someone else was with him.

Full of excitement, Senn climbed on board and entered the dimly lit cabin where the smiling face of Stephan greeted him. And peeping out from behind him stood the teary-eyed, beaming Laura.

CHAPTER 48

THE PRECIOUS PICKUP

"When a man is pushed, tormented, defeated, he has a chance to learn something."

—RALPH WALDO EMERSON

Tears rolling down her cheeks, Laura rushed past Stephan, wrapped her arms tightly around Senn, and wept with unbridled joy. Senn held her tight as tears gushed out from him and choked all his words. Reuniting with his best friend was his singular dream in Venice, and it had come true.

The world stopped its endless spin, and everything felt pristine and complete for a moment.

Laura kept crying as she pulled back and said in a halting voice, "I am so happy to see you, Nico. You have no idea how much I've prayed to meet you. Especially on the island, that evil man showed up out of nowhere and, at gunpoint, tied us and threatened to cut us into pieces! I thought we would die until you appeared and saved our lives." Laura wiped her tears with her sleeve and looked at Senn's bandages, then glanced back at Stephan and asked in a worried tone, "Stephan said you were in the hospital. Did you get hurt? God! We have so much to talk about but so little time."

Laura held Senn's hand, led him to the seats in the cabin, and sat next to Stephan. She looked happy and excited even though the rest of her face and body told a different story.

Dark circles imprisoned her free-spirited blue eyes. She'd lost a lot of weight, and the protruding veins on her neck amplified the anxiety in her voice when she spoke. Her crumpled clothes hung on her body like a scarecrow. The large diamond wedding ring (the only proof of her newfound joy) rolled perilously around her bony finger as she gesticulated wildly, offloading her worry to Senn.

But underneath all this surface trauma, Senn could still feel the optimistic, never-give-in/give-up girl he knew as her blazing eyes darted between Stephan and Senn, her two favorite men in the world.

Stephan looked haggard as well as he shook Senn's hand vigorously and said, "I'm sorry, Senn, to ask you to come like this, but we had to meet you."

Senn nodded, winked, and replied, "Apart from dodging two police guards snoring outside my front door, the trip was a breeze."

Stephan and Laura chuckled as Laura beamed at Senn and gave him another big squeeze. Stephan, in the meantime, restarted the engine and turned the boat into the canal, heading into the city's center under cover of the quilt-like surface fog over the icy waters.

Stephan turned serious and said, "I know you have many questions, but you need to believe me when I say we can't trust anyone right now. No one."

Laura chipped in, sounding exasperated and looking at Senn, "Yes, Stephan is right, Nico. The mafia owns the police."

Puzzled, Senn asked, "How did this all start?"

Laura, looking anxious, recalled, "I was at the wrong place at the wrong time."

"No one knew we were dating," began Laura, glancing lovingly at Stephan. "I used to wait for him after the rehearsals to come down to the basement where Stephan had a private studio. That was our love nest." Laura giggled as she stressed the word *nest* a bit more than usual. Senn could see Stephan was a bit embarrassed yet enjoying Laura unveiling their little secret.

Laura continued, "We were madly in love, but Stephan was worried his mother might take issue with our affair. Mia hated any woman who liked him. She had a superstition that Stephan's life could be in danger if he married the wrong woman."

Lauren sighed. "We never told her. And now we wish we had."

Senn had guessed right. Mia did not know about Laura and Stephan.

Laura's voice turned anxious. "But one night, I was waiting for Stephan to show up when I heard some voices outside. I'd never heard anyone in the basement before, so I stepped out saw a man choking a woman. I never saw his face, just his tall, bony frame, and ponytail."

She continued after a pause, "I was so shocked, I screamed and ran out, but I knew he saw me. I looked back one last time and saw the woman lying on the floor, unconscious. I was sure she was dead. And the man had disappeared. "

Laura stopped talking, and her hollow, scared eyes stared at Senn, speechless and traumatized by the memory.

Noticing Laura's pain, Stephan stepped up. "And that's when he began to harass us. I did not know who he was, Senn. I used to get calls from him on my phone in the middle of the night asking about Laura and how he wanted to meet her alone. I never dealt with the mafia directly; just the boat captain Luca, who ferried goods in and out of the basement." Stephan continued, " I had a huge dilemma.

Laura knew nothing about who the man was and what he was doing in the basement." Stephan paused as he slowed his boat and switched on his fog lamps.

The visibility was getting worse. Senn wanted to ask where they were going, but Stephan spoke again.

"I had not yet told Laura about the deal with the mafia or the cocaine. I was afraid she would get scared and leave me."

Stephan sighed as he glanced lovingly at Laura and continued, "So I hid her in the Ottagono and begged her to stop all contact with the outer world until I could get us all out of there. But then this bastard somehow found us."

Senn interjected, "But why didn't you tell me about Antonio when we met?"

Stephan's face went crimson, and he replied, "Antonio threatened to kill my mother if I told anyone. And I knew there was a mole in Taino's force. I could not tell you and risk you mentioning it to Taino. Also, I had to let the mafia believe that Laura was genuinely missing to push any suspicions away from me, keep Laura safe, and give me the time I needed to plan my getaway."

Senn glanced at Laura, who was calmly looking at Stephan, and she added, "Yes, I was shocked when he told me what was going on in the Teatro. But alas, I loved him by then!" Laura leaned over and kissed Stephan and flashed a beaming smile.

Senn smiled at the couple. "I guess, Stephan, you took Laura from your private mooring under the Teatro straight to the Ottagano, hidden under your seat, and returned the boat to where it was. How were you so sure Luca or Dario would not find out?"

Stephan smiled, looking impressed. "Yes. I knew the taxi's worked usually till 1 AM and then stayed parked from 1-3 every night until the drugs shunted from 3-5 AM. So I moved Laura when the taxis were idle. So neither Luca nor Dario knew anything about my plans."

Senn smiled at the couple, looked at Stephan, and asked, "And why did you say Laura heard a ghost the first time we met? That confused me!

Stephan smiled at Laura and then turned to Senn. "I exaggerated to make Laura sound loony."

Laura giggled and replied, "Yes, it was Stephan's way to muddy the waters for the Police."

Stephan shrugged and smiled. "I got that from my mother. She used to say she heard voices down there, but I never heard anything."

Senn suddenly realized Mia had taken her dark secret to the grave. Neither Stephan nor Laura had any idea of what she'd done.

Senn decided to leave it like that.

Stephan slowed the boat, moored outside a church, and turned to Senn. "You'll need to wait here with Laura. I need to go inside and get something."

Senn nodded and glanced at Laura, who looked worried as Stephan exited the boat, dashed into the side entrance of the church, and disappeared inside.

Senn, stunned, asked, "Where's he gone?"

Laura replied quietly, "To pick up the Modigliani."

CHAPTER 49

THE CUNNING PLAN

"When you go in search of honey,
you must expect to be stung by bees."

—JOSEPH JOUBERT

In the chilly darkness, Laura and Senn waited for Stephan to re-emerge from behind the opaque church doors. The fog was thickening over the icy canal waters, reducing the visibility to only a few meters.

Senn stared at Laura for a moment, then said, "Laura, you need to listen to me carefully. I know Col. Taino, the head of the Venetian police. The mafia tried to kill him, too, so he's in hiding now. He asked me to try and convince you both *or you by yourself* to surrender to his team and let them protect you. I think you can trust him. I can vouch for that."

In a calm, determined tone, Laura shook her head and replied, "I can't, Nico. I can't. He's the love of my life. He risked his life to smuggle me out in his boat that night from the Teatro to the Ottogano. He kept us a secret to protect me. He did not budge even after they threatened to kill Mia. His life's in more danger than mine, and I can't leave him now."

Senn tried again, this time with more urgency in his voice.

"Laura, let me convince him to go to Col. Taino. I'm telling you, he's trustworthy. He's on our side. I am sure we can all trust him."

This time, Laura shook her head harder and moved back a few inches from Senn. "It's not the police chief we don't trust. You may be right. But there are moles in his inner circle that we dread. Even Taino can't find them." Laura's eyes darted between Senn and the church door as she spoke in an anxious voice, "Nico, I've made this mistake once, and it got Mia killed. I forced Stephan to call Taino and warn him about the mole in his force who wanted to kill him. And the same day, they attacked him. I can't risk that happening to Stephan again. We have a plan and want to tell you about it as soon as we have the painting in our hands."

Senn could tell Laura was inconvincible.

Senn felt looped out of the couple's plans now. He'd agreed to meet them explicitly to convince them to surrender to Col. Taino and gain protection under the witness program. But this was not what the two wanted. They were determined to pilot their destiny, no matter the risk.

Senn heard a shuffle, and they both turned to see Stephan's dark outline rushing back towards the boat. He was panting with thick vapor gushing from his mouth as he stumbled into the cabin, eyes blazing, and in his hand, he carried a small, leather violin case. Jubilant, he looked at Laura and exclaimed, "Freedom, baby! Freedom!"

As Laura and Stephan hugged and kissed each other passionately like a couple of teens in love, Senn waited for them to speak. They looked overwhelmed at their find.

Senn was sure it was the same painting he'd seen in the Teatro basement.

Stephan turned to Senn and said, "Mr. Senn, this is our ticket to freedom. Inside is my mother's Modigliani. I hid it behind the alter. It's what you saw that first night you came to the Teatro basement."

Senn nodded and, with a chuckle, replied, "I remember how angry you got at my discovery of it."

Stephan smiled. "Yes, I was hiding it there from the mafia as my insurance policy in case something went wrong with our arrangement, as it now has! It's the last painting Modigliani did before leaving Venice."

He pointed to the vintage violin case and said, "I smuggled the painting to this church just before I flooded the basement to deceive the police and their mafia informants."

Senn nodded. "What are you planning to do with it?"

Stephan paused to answer as he fired the engine up and steered the boat back into the heavily fogged canal, casting a surreal spell on the surroundings.

Stephan kept his eyes on the water and replied, "I have an agent in Istanbul who will help us sell it."

"How much do you hope to get from the sale?"

Stephan checked with Laura, who nodded and replied, "It's worth over $100,000,000." He paused, let the number sink in, and added, "I hope we'll get half that in the black market."

Senn whistled with disbelief and chuckled. "So, this is your plan. Disappear into the fog with $100,000,000 masterpiece in a violin case?"

Stephan, instead of smiling, looked blankly at Senn and replied, "Well, we were hoping you could join us."

Senn looked stunned and a bit confused as he waited for Stephan to explain.

Stephan kept his eyes on the water, steering the boat slowly out into the open waters and heading towards Lido Island.

Then he looked at Senn and said, "Laura and I have a plane waiting in Lido to fly us out to Zagreb, and then we're driving to Istanbul, and we would love it if you joined us."

Laura, who'd been quiet so far, added in an urgent, pleading voice, "Nico, you must come with us. We have it all planned. Your life is in danger here, and you can't stay in Venice any longer. Taino is powerless now. He's lost control of the mafia in Venice."

Senn was not expecting this. It was a tempting offer. He would gain his freedom while ensuring they were both out of danger.

He could see why this plan made sense for the couple. Laura was not going to leave Stephan behind. Even though this exposed her to harm in the future, at least she would be with Stephan and have a chance to reconstruct a comfortable, anonymous life with him.

As the fog thinned, Stephan stepped on the gas and raced towards the private airport on Lido island.

Senn smiled at the couple and pondered his options as Venice melted in the wake behind them.

CHAPTER 50

GASPING FOR HELP

As Stephan slowly moored the boat into the Lido airport through the heavy snowfall, Senn spotted a couple of police officers in the harbor, keenly observing their arrival.

Senn motioned to Stephan, who grimly nodded that he'd also noticed. Laura looked worried as the policemen suspiciously stared at the boat while talking to each other.

The impending confrontation made Senn uncomfortable. None of them were innocent tourists on a family holiday. They were hunted and wanted people while on Venetian soil. As if reading his mind, Stephan pulled out a blue pouch from his backpack, handed Senn a brown envelope from inside, and said, "I got this made, hoping you might join us."

Senn opened it and found a British passport with his faded photograph and the name *Robert Manning*. It was a brilliant forgery. The document looked old and used, with multiple immigration stamps and his youthful face from college staring back at him.

Senn looked surprised and said, "Wow! That's quite a forgery. How did you manage that?"

Stephan winked at Laura, who smiled at Senn and said, "We've been planning this for a while, Nico. Even before I saw Antonio killing that girl. But when you arrived looking for me, we just added you to the list."

Laura stood. I'm Julia Manning, your sister."

And Stephan chipped in, "I am Marc Webber from Luxembourg, Julia's fiancé and your brother-in-law-to-be."

All three beamed at each other, acknowledging each other's new avatar and, for a moment, enjoying the feeling of being the only family they had left.

A few minutes later, Marc, Julia, and Robert stepped into the sparse airport building, approached the police desk, greeted the officers, and handed them their IDs.

The officers behind the desk looked suspiciously at them. But before they could say much, Stephan turned on his charm and told them he was flying his fiancé and her brother to a friend's wedding in Zagreb, where he was the best man, and how he was worried they would not make it in time and how he had the poor groom's ring with him. The officers seemed entertained by Stephan's hysterics and calmed down. He let them through, and then the second officer looked at Senn's bandaged face and queried the cause. Senn told him he'd been in a car accident but was lucky to be alive.

The officer stared at Senn, then squinted at his passport a bit longer, looked over at his fellow officer, and whispered something Senn didn't catch.

Senn's blood pressure rose while Stephan and Laura stood on the other side of the glass door, looking nervous. The officer took another hard look at the picture on the passport, then at Senn, and finally asked in a low voice, "You an actor, Mr. Manning?"

Senn smiled and shook his head. "Not guilty, sir."

Disarmed by Senn's sense of humor, the officer smiled, handed back the passport, and let him through.

As Senn went through security, he removed Laura's backpack under his jacket and handed it to a surprised Laura.

Senn hugged her and whispered, "Couldn't let you leave without your old faithful. The key and the bracelet are in the inside pocket."

Laura blushed. "Thank you. I had a feeling you'd find them. Stephan gifted both of them to me."

Stephan winked at Senn as the three briskly made their way to the back of the building and met the pilot, who suggested an hour's delay until the weather improved.

While happy to be leaving with Laura and Stephan, Senn kept thinking about Anna as he sat in the waiting room.

The last time they'd spoken was more than a day ago, and she'd been worried about him even then. Senn checked his phone and realized he'd switched it off before meeting Laura and Stephan.

He switched it back on and, using a GPS spoofer, teleported his location to his new flat before checking his messages.

He saw Anna had sent him a single message that read, "I'm in trouble."

Her subsequent text confirmed his dread.

It read, "I think they're outside the house. Help me!"

Senn stepped away from Laura and Stephan and called her. The phone rang for a few seconds, and Anna picked up. She sounded scared as she spoke.

"Senn, where are you? I can't get hold of Uncle T. I think someone's been outside the house for the last few minutes, and another car just arrived. I'm scared, Senn."

Senn didn't have much time. The GPS scrambler was secure for approximately a minute, but its shield could leak after that, and he couldn't compromise Laura and Stephan's location.

He lied, aligned himself to the fake location lock that the GPS was set to, and said, "I'm at my flat. Where's your security?"

"He's not answering his phone; I've tried calling many times," she replied in an anxious, cracking voice. "I think he's dead."

After a pause, she said in a tired, helpless voice, "What should I do? Can you come here? There's another car outside now. I'm scared, Senn."

Without thinking, Senn said, "Send me your location. Can you hide somewhere? And keep trying Taino. I'm on my way."

Her location pin came in. He clicked on it and saw it was on Lido itself!

He had no idea she lived in Lido.

Or maybe she'd mentioned it, and he'd not paid attention. The place was on the south side, close to Alberoni, about 5 kilometers south of where he was.

Senn's mind was racing as he sorted through the options. It was almost 6.30 in the morning but still pitch dark outside. He could drive out and bring her back in less than 30 minutes.

He turned and saw Stephan and Laura's worried faces staring at him. Stephan asked who that was, and Senn explained the situation to them.

Laura and Stephan looked at each other and silently nodded. Stephan turned to Senn with an empathetic look and asked, "Do you trust her?"

"Absolutely," replied Senn.

"Then go and get her. My car's in the parking lot, no. D7, the keys are in front of the front right tire. We'll wait for you for an hour. We've got an extra seat on the plane. She can have that."

Senn nodded, gave both of them a big hug, and promised to return in time. He knew the trip could be lethal but couldn't leave Anna in trouble.

As he was out the door, Senn turned to Stephan and Laura and said, "It's 6.30 right now. If I'm not back by 7.30, promise me you'll leave?"

They grudgingly nodded and waved goodbye as Laura started crying.

CHAPTER 51

THE LAST MILE DASH

"The best way to rescue a world with hurting people is to do it one person at a time."

—MANUEL CORAZZARI

Senn knew he was risking his life as he sped out of the parking lot in Stephan's Maserati, heading towards a distraught Anna.

He had 55 minutes to find her, outsmart the mafia, get back to the airport with her, and fly out with Stephan and Laura.

Senn floored the accelerator with one eye on his phone. The location pin suggested the place was 6 minutes away. The car skidded a few times due to the ice, but Senn was relentless. In his mind, the biggest hurdle was decoying the goons away from Anna's place.

He sent her a voice text, "6 minutes away. You OK?"

An instant text reply came back, "Yes. Hurry. They're trying to unlock the door."

Senn felt her panic; he asked, "Did you reach Taino?"

She replied, "Yes, he's sending his men now."

The road turned off the main road and climbed onto a dirt track heading for the dunes. This was the old, industrial area of the island and was used mainly for ship repairs and dismantling—not the usual residential area of Lido.

But Senn expected Anna to live off the grid given her daredevil, independent personality. They'd never spoken about their families ever. There was never enough time. He knew very little about her personal life besides the fact she was Col. Taino's niece who dreamt of becoming a cop.

Senn reached the top of the road and saw the dirt road ended, replaced by a snowed knoll sloping down towards the ocean. Senn looked at the map to be sure. It showed he was still 500 meters from the destination, but there was no road ahead. Confused, he switched the engine off and checked his phone. Anna's texts had gone silent.

Are you OK? Senn texted.

He waited for a few seconds and saw no reply.

Senn looked at the snow on the ground and spotted motorcycle-tread marks going over the hill. Senn, on a hunch, switched off his GPS scrambler and left Col. Taino a voice text giving his precise location.

Going to Anna's house. Send help fast.

And switched his scrambler back on and rechecked his messages.

Nothing.

Senn looked at his watch as he got out of the car and sprinted down the hill.

6.45 AM.

He'd not anticipated walking the last few hundred meters. The only light source available to him was the glow of his phone as he spotted an enclave of small warehouses in the distance.

Senn rechecked his phone for a message from Anna and saw she'd left him a voice message.

He winced as he heard her scared, whispering voice come on, and she said,

"I'm in the basement. I can hear them upstairs. Come to the black door at the back. Find the lock at the base. The code is 1703. Take the stairs down. I am hiding in the tool shed."

Senn stepped up his pace. A few meters ahead, the road turned sharply, and right in front of him was the solitary converted warehouse where the phone trail ended. It was one of those shabby, chic loft-style conversions with a stunning ocean view.

Mature cypress and pine trees shrouded the approach, but Senn spotted a pickup truck and a couple of bikes outside. The lights upstairs were on, but Senn couldn't see anyone inside.

Senn snaked his way to the back and saw a large-wheeled, industrial loader parked in the backyard. As he approached the house, he picked up the muffled sound of a male voice in the room above. It was a gruff voice speaking to someone in a foreign language.

Then a few seconds later, he heard two other voices.

A gust of fear paralyzed Senn for a second. He was sure they were heavily armed. He desperately needed more time planning his entry.

But time was also against him. He had to keep moving.

He tiptoed to the black door, felt for the lock with his fingers, and found it at its foot. He rolled the digits of the code, but it did not respond. Senn tried again. 1703.

He heard a click and, to his relief, opened without making a sound.

It was almost 7 AM. He had to get out of there in the next 10 minutes with Anna to have any chance of catching that plane.

Senn slowly pushed the door open while checking for any sounds. He could still hear the men upstairs but nothing on the ground floor.

Senn stepped inside the pitch-dark space and waited for his eyes to adjust to the darkness.

He pulled out his phone and saw there was a message from Anna.

It read, "I think they found me."

Before Senn could react to the heart-breaking text, he heard a couple of loud gunshots from the basement. Senn's heart sank.

Just then, something hard pushed into his back, and a voice shouted, "Don't move, mother fucker."

The next second he felt a stinging pain as a heavy object whacked him over his head. Senn's legs buckled, and he fell to the ground.

Senn tried hard to stay conscious, but his eyes blurred and blacked out.

The last words he heard before passing out was a man shouting, "You're a dead man, Senn!"

CHAPTER 52

V.I.P SENN

"Do not be afraid of what should be afraid of you."

—CONSTANCE FRIDAY

Senn jerked back into consciousness to the sound of distressed bleating goats around him. The blindfolds hid the rest.

From the sounds and smells, he could tell he was lying on the floor of a moving truck full of scared goats. The tight blindfold cord cut into his aching ears and magnified the mind-numbing pain in his head. He could smell stale urine and cow dung from the heavy, wet tarpaulin lying over his body. His mouth was tightly duct taped, and his hands and feet were firmly metal-cuffed, digging into his wrists and ankles like serrated razor blades.

Senn reckoned the truck was semi-open as icy winds flooded the cramped space, freezing his nose and thirsty, chapped lips. The vehicle's slow, winding ascent over the unmetalled road made his stomach churn, making him want to throw up. The lurching truck took its first toll within a few minutes as he coughed up vile vomit all over his face and neck.

The only consolation to his helplessness was the heat from the screaming engine that leaked through the metal walls and warmed the back of his body.

Senn had no clue how long he'd been unconscious.

His last memory was being clubbed hard over his head, and a man barked into his face as he fainted. He also recalled the heart-wrenching text from Anna and hearing gunshots as her hideout got compromised.

Senn felt gutted for not being able to save her life but hopeful that Laura and Stephan had flown out of Italy safely.

One thing that did surprise him *a bit* was that he was still alive.

The people he was messing with did not like taking prisoners. It was a tedious and bad business practice to keep men who did not matter alive.

The road trip was also confusing.

Why move him out? From the sounds of the road and the incline, Senn was sure he was out of Venice. No streets and altitudes like this were in Venice or any of the surrounding islands. And being transported in a livestock truck said he was in a hilly rural area where this kind of freight would not be out of character.

The only reasonable explanation he could muster was that someone wanted a long, undisturbed chat with him.

This VIP treatment worried Senn.

The bleating of the goats dimmed as the truck ground to a halt on the dirt track. Senn stiffened as he heard men speaking in a strange foreign language from inside the truck. They seemed to be arguing about something. After a few seconds, the truck door flew open, and one of the men jumped out, and Senn heard the bonnet opening.

From all the commotion, it seemed they had engine trouble. The second man got off the truck and walked to the back of the vehicle, sending the goats into a terror tizzy. The man shouted menacingly at the terrified animals to shut up, making the poor animals feel worse as they stamped around, trying their hardest to stay as far away as possible from the man. Senn's body rocked as some of them banged and rattled his wooden cage.

Then he heard his name.

"Senn! You bastard," barked the man in a heavy accent.

Senn lay still and pretended to be unconscious.

The voice rasped again, "Don't die yet, you dog. You're the star of the party!"

And then the man howled with laughter as the terrified goats bleated in fear.

Senn lay still as the man walked a few feet away from the truck and urinated while the second man filled water into the sizzling hot radiator. From how they confidently walked around, Senn could tell it was daylight outside. Then he heard another vehicle approaching and slowing beside them. The men walked up, and Senn heard someone address the men in Croatian. The men answered in Italian, and after a bit of banter, the vehicle sped away.

Senn had his first bearings. He was somewhere in Croatia.

He tried to estimate the distance. If this was the same day since his capture, he was at least 400 kms out of Venice, headed south along the Adriatic Sea. And Senn knew that could mean only one thing. He was heading towards Albania.

The mecca of the cocaine underworld.

Not a place he'd planned to visit. Especially not blindfolded and in chains.

CHAPTER 53

FAMILIAR FOES

The truck resumed its circuitous incline over tortuous roads while Senn made sense of his predicament inside his suffocating cell surrounded by panicked goats.

Now he knew two men were escorting him. But the scary part was being called *the star of the party*.

What party? Was it a euphemism for protracted torture on arrival? He knew the Albanians were active in the Venice cocaine underworld, but he'd not come across them. So far.

Senn knew the Albanian mafia was supplying cocaine to the Italians but did not realize they were involved with Stephan. He recalled seeing some articles in the local press discussing the rise of Albanian drivers and boat and gondola skippers in the last couple of years. Maybe it was a cover-up to hide their true intent—to smuggle cocaine in and out of Venice.

Anyhow, Senn focused on his immediate alternatives to keep panic at bay.

The last time he was in a coffin-like cell like this was a couple of years ago in Egypt while covering the story of the illegal tomb raiding going on there. After the military betrayed him, the smugglers (as a kind of morbid joke) caged him in a coffin and left him to die in the scorching desolate desert with a ticking bomb strapped to his chest.

By an insane stroke of luck, the bomb had failed to detonate, and a passing caravan had set him free.

But this one was harder.

He felt weak and disoriented like some hallucinogenic was in him to impede retaliation, and all his thoughts circled back to one thing again and again.

Water. He was going mad with thirst.

He could taste the blood from his parched, cracked lips on and off, which dampened his craving ever so slightly, and the blindfold was so tight that it was making his ears ring in pain.

He needed to distract himself.

At moments like this, Senn reverted to a mind control practice, focusing all his attention on a single sound or sensation outside his discomfort. The exercise helped to separate him from his obstacles in a productive way, eventually leading to some way forward or solution.

Senn decided to turn his attention to the breathing of his fellow captives—the goats.

To get the best angle on their sounds, he pushed his head and nose into the wood until he could smell it and realized it was cheap, fresh wood planks nailed together—the kind used to transport freight.

Senn had an idea. He slowly rubbed his head against the inside, hoping for spikes or nails to help him dislodge or loosen the blindfolds. There was nothing on one side. He turned his head and tried to find something on the other side.

This time he felt a small prick on his forehead, and his hopes flared. He felt a protruding nail, which felt long enough to be the anchor for him to rip or move the cloth off if he hooked into his blindfold. But the risk was that the nail could tear into his skin and add to his pain. But under the circumstances, he was determined to try.

Senn pushed his head into the nail until it sufficiently pierced the blindfold and started to move it off his face. He now had a sole focus. Keep the blindfold hooked until it dislodged.

Senn could feel his plan working despite the pain of the nail gashing his forehead. After a few minutes of careful head-butting and pushing, the blindfold slipped over Senn's forehead, letting light blind him for the first time.

God damn it. He could see!

He felt a massive surge of relief as he feasted his eyes on the sliver of sunlight sneaking through a single crack in his cask. He could see the bobbing heads of goats in the truck tightly huddled together, obstructing the vast, snowy, mountainous terrain in the background. The thick, smelly tarpaulin cover over his box blocked all other visibility.

Senn tried to use the same nail to remove the gag over his mouth, but it was too far, and there was no wiggle room to move in the box. He had to wait to solve that problem.

Senn stiffened when the truck slowed again. It had climbed to the top of the mountain and reached a plateau. The goats had woken and looked restless as they stamped and shuffled in the truck as if sensing something ominous. This time the two men did not come out, but Senn could hear one of them speaking to someone on the phone, again in a foreign language he'd never heard before. Then the man hung up, jumped out of the truck, and walked in front of the vehicle.

Senn went still and listened intently. He could feel the biting wind on his face as it shook the truck with its intensity at the high altitude. But then he heard the distant sound of approaching vehicles. The goats began bleating nervously again. The sound of the engines grew louder, and Senn could tell it was more than one vehicle as they slowed next to their parked truck.

His escorts spoke to the new people with deference in muted voices.

Heavy footsteps approached the back of the truck, and through the crack, Senn saw three tall, heavy-built men staring at the goats and his box. The goats receded in fear, obscuring Senn's view.

One of the men shouted instructions, and a metal ramp offloaded the panicked goats. Then two men climbed up; one lifted the tarp off the box and looked inside. Through the slats, Senn saw a burly, white man's dark, fierce eyes staring down with a gun pointed at him.

Senn recognized the man instantly. It was Mikkey, the police officer in Col. Taino's office.

CHAPTER 54

THE GOOD IS OFT SHATTERED WITH THE BONES

"Given total power over another, the human being will find that his thoughts turn to torture."

—MARTIN AMIS

The burly cop scowled down at Senn and, without uttering a word, smashed his fist into him.

Senn yelped as his nose exploded in pain. The man paused long enough to admire his damage, then calmly refixed the blindfold over his eyes and re-draped the tarp, leaving him in freezing darkness.

Then a few seconds later, two men jumped into the revving truck, which skidded down the mountain road at a ragged pace.

Fear swamped Senn while his body dealt with the ferocity and suddenness of the blow, and his mind digested, finally confronting Col. Taino's dirty mole.

Everyone called him Mikkey, Senn recalled as he tried to jigsaw more details about the rogue cop. He'd seen him whenever he came to the station to meet the colonel but never paid much attention to him.

Senn remembered he'd bumped into the same guy on the day of the bomb blast in the police station. Even though that day's events were sketchy, there was something odd about this guy. He was dressed in a fashionable, all-white civilian suit and escorting his girlfriend, who kept staring at him and Anna as they passed. Senn remembered this detail because the woman had an unusually thick tattoo all around her neck, like an embroidered dog collar that stood out in her off-shoulder, white dress.

As the truck descended the mountain at high speed, Senn sensed they were approaching the ocean as the cold air now smelled of salt and stale sardines.

The truck reached a forested area, and Senn smelled pine and eucalyptus around them. The vehicle stopped briefly before a heavy metal gate slowly opened to let them through. They drove for a few hundred meters, then the sound changed and began to resound like they were going over cobbled stones in a tunnel. After about a minute of driving, the truck came to a dead halt, and Senn felt the sounds of his box unlocking and the rough hands yanking him up on his feet.

The long journey had stiffened his shackled legs into a pulp, and he buckled the second his feet touched the ground.

The men gruffly propped him up and dragged him down a cold hallway that felt like a dungeon until they reached a room where some other people were waiting. He could hear the chime of chains and metal rods getting ready to welcome him.

Senn was too weak to resist, but he was sure he was being prepared for torture by the smell of sweat, urine, and blood from dirty clothes and clogged toilet bowls around him.

One of the men strapped a leather harness around his chest, and a metal hook slotted into his back that instantly lifted him off his feet. Then the flurry of activity suddenly ceased like a symphony awaiting its crescendo.

Then the room exploded and reverberated with a loud motor, and a pressure washer with freezing water slashed into Senn's body like a samurai sword.

Senn hated cold showers.

After what seemed like a lifetime under a glacier, the water stopped, leaving a shivering Senn to dry off to the sounds of his chattering teeth.

Senn was tired, scared, and yet curious. Why did someone want to take so much effort to torture him like this? He was not so valuable to any mafia—neither the Venetian nor the Albanian.

This treatment felt personal. Like someone was enjoying enforcing the pain for the sake of the pleasure from it.

Then he heard footsteps, and someone stood behind him, slowly untied his blindfold, and ungagged his mouth. The fingers were soft, and the person doing it seemed to linger on each action for just that second longer.

The cold, sodden gags fell to the floor, and Senn momentarily enjoyed his first ungagged breath since Venice.

CHAPTER 55

DOV'È STEFANO?

Senn was too weak to resist the two masked men who forced his arms and legs out like a Vitruvian man and cuffed them to heavy chains on the floor and ceiling. Then they gruffly got rid of his clothes with jagged-edged scissors and left, leaving him naked and soaking wet in the middle of a frigid room.

He'd faced dead ends before, and this felt like a Biggy.

His muscles tensed, dreading the next onslaught of pain, but the place fell silent. He could hear his shallow breath intertwined with his chattering teeth in the eerie darkness.

Every hair on his body wanted to scream out in rage, but he resisted because that would signal defeat in the eyes of his captors. He knew that from here on, his only hope of surviving was not through strength and endurance but with a steely mind. It was going to be a game of non-compliance, deflection, and silence against the brute aggression of the enemy.

His body would most likely fail him, but his mind was untouchable.

So instead of fretting about the unknown, Senn set his mind to hatching an escape.

Senn tugged hard at the chains, making his muscles burn, but found them stubbornly firm. He looked around the room and observed the rugged, faded, white walls speckled with a spray of dark blotches. He didn't linger too long on the cause of the stains as a long, red nylon rope dangling from the ceiling with a noose tied to its end magnetized his gaze and made him shudder.

It was a death camp with interludes of torture.

He knew he was somewhere on the Albanian coast from all the signs along the way, but he needed a more precise location to map his options.

Just then, a chair creaked behind him.

There was someone else in the room.

Before he could sense who it was, the room resounded with the deafening sound of church bells that lasted for twelve strikes, marking midnight.

Senn waited for the sound to rinse off the walls before concentrating on the other person he'd felt a moment ago. He raised his voice and asked, "Who's there? Talk to me."

He waited for a response, but there was none. Maybe it was his mind playing tricks with him. But suddenly, he heard a rustle of cloth as someone stood and began walking towards him.

The shoes of the person approaching made a strange metallic sound as they moved. Like a boot with a metal tassel rubbing against each other.

The person walked calmly, came up, stood a few feet behind him, paused, and turned a switch that flooded a blinding halogen light on Senn's face, making him slam his eyes shut in reflex.

Before he could adjust to the light, a cold rod touched his back, and Senn shrieked as a high-voltage current shot through his body. It was high enough to make Senn dizzy and nauseous. He'd been struck by lightning before, and this brought back the stinging memory.

He could feel the person enjoying the shock's impact on his body. The footsteps behind him moved forward again as Senn gritted his teeth for the next blow. It landed on his neck and made his head rock like a pack of coiled springs as he convulsed in pain and smelt the stench of burnt hair in his nostrils. Senn knew the voltage on the rod was potentially lethal. He just prayed it was not how they intended to finish him.

Senn's legs buckled as he started drifting into unconsciousness due to the force of the current. But just then, he felt the sting of a whiplash across his back that made him careen forward and shock him back to consciousness.

Senn started frothing from his mouth and nose at the intensity of the injuries, and each breath came out as a long, strenuous wheeze while the halogen light temporarily blinded him

Then, just like that, the person switched off the halogen, and everything adorned the cloak of silence again.

Senn gasped for breath and wept softly to comfort himself and quicken his recovery before the next onslaught. He was not sure how long he would last.

The person behind him stood motionless as Senn groaned and slashed around, trying to reduce the intensity of the ache. But then, he swooped forward and stood right up next to Senn, and their bodies touched for the first time.

Senn froze, anticipating a strike but instead felt the cold leather of the person's jacket on his bare back, and there was something else. He felt straight, long hair brush his neck and shoulders.

Then he felt moist lips and warm breath on his ear, and a woman's tantalizing whisper said, *"Dov'è Stefano?"*

The words *and how she said them* made Senn freeze in total confusion. *Impossible*, he shrieked in his head.

It can't be.

It can't be.

But it sounded *just like* Anna.

The woman seemed unperturbed and repeated the question, but this time placed a cold, sharp blade on Senn's testicles and, with an added excitement in her voice, said, *"Dov'è Stefano, Senn?"*

It *was* Anna.

He waited to recover from his shock and grief and, in a halting voice, asked, "Anna?"

From here on, the consequences for Senn were frightening.

CHAPTER 56

CONFESSING TO THE CONVICT

The woman froze and repelled away from Senn when he called her Anna.

She cleared her throat as if to begin speaking but halted. Instead, she walked away, picked up the chair, and turned a switch that lit up a small, naked bulb over Senn's head.

The footsteps returned, and she walked past Senn without looking at him (her face still shrouded by her jet-black, ramrod hair), placed her chair a few feet away, sat with her head down, and replied, in a somber tone, *"Yes, it's me, Senn."*

Then she raised her head and glared at Senn for the first time.

His hair stood on end as he gasped in recognition.

God damn it! It was Anna. But wasn't she dead?

He'd heard distinct gunshots fired that night he went to rescue her. This woman had to be a fake.

Senn kept staring at her. She was unlike any Anna he knew.

Not Anna, his relentless, sincere partner, studiously aiding his search for Laura. Not Anna, the cheerful, inquisitive gum-totting apprentice. Not Anna, the concerned, worried friend for his entire time in Venice.

This Anna was demonic with a smoldering, serpentine aura.

She'd lost some weight. Her high cheekbones jutted against her thin, pale skin, and dark circles formed whirlpools around her glassy, opaque eyes. Her all-black attire of jeans and leather jacket accentuated the stygian transformation.

And her hair was nothing like he'd last seen on her. Gone were the thick, wavy, light brown frizzes. Instead, she'd adorned a stern, sheer look and dyed her hair jet-black. The matching smoky eyebrows tapered on the ends added to her piercing, ruthless stare.

She sat across from a chained, naked Senn, slowly lit a cigarette, and took a long, deep drag. Then flicked the burning matchstick at Senn in contempt and anger.

Then she leaned back on the metal chair, unzipped her jacket, revealing two Glock 17 pistols in her cloak shoulder holster, crossed her legs over her knee-high, white embroidered leather boots, and spoke.

"OK. Let's finish this. For the last time, where's Stephan?" she asked in a low, menacing voice.

Senn kept staring back at her, unsure if she was Anna. Then in a low whisper, replied, "No clue."

Then after a pause, Senn continued, this time in a suspicious tone, " Who are you? Anna's dead."

The woman smiled wryly and replied, "I came back from the dead to hunt you down, Senn." She smirked and continued, "That night when I texted you to come over and *save me*, I knew you were with Stephan and Laura. We were ready for you all at Basilica Santa Maria, but all you bastards disappeared. We moved the team to my place, hoping my desperate call for help would make you come. We faked the gunshots and the messages to depress you."

Then she made a mocking gesture of sympathy and quipped, "And the rest is geography."

This time, Senn had to concede defeat. She was the only person who knew the meeting point with Stephan and Laura that night.

Senn fell silent. The blow of betrayal knocked the wind out of him as he slumped into the chains and hung his head in shock and sadness.

He was so disappointed, mostly at himself for not clocking that Anna was the queen mole in Taino's police force.

But why? The question kept firing in his mind. Why would Anna, the niece of Col. Taino, an aspiring cop, be part of the mafia, and Why did she care about arresting Stephan? What else was she hiding?

He had to prize it all out of her. But he had to be patient and play with her ego to make her reveal her plumes.

After another deep puff, Anna narrowed her gaze at Senn. "You know, Senn, I was your first follower when you started your YouTube channel. I even wrote a paper in college about some of the cases you'd uncovered. So when I heard you were coming to Venice, I had to work with you."

She carefully blew some cigarette ash off her boots. She continued, "I convinced Uncle Taino, who, by the way, has no idea who I am, that I needed a criminal investigation project for my thesis."

Anna giggled, lowered her eyes shyly, and said, "I even told him I was a big fan of your work. Sweet Uncle, pity he started getting too nosey about Stephan and the Teatro business. The cartel wanted him dead anyway for the heavy losses he'd caused them. But I was trying to be a protective niece."

Senn raised his eyebrow and asked, "So you planted the bomb in the station?"

Anna chuckled. "Not me. You did, silly. Remember the chocolates you carried to his room? That was the bomb with your DNA and fingerprints all over the bag."

She smiled proudly and ran her fingers through her hair while Senn tried to avoid her stare to hide his disgust.

"But why?" blurted Senn. "Why did you want to kill your uncle? He adored you!"

Anna shut her eyes, looking exasperated. "Because my family wanted me to. Maybe you still don't get it, Senn," she said, sounding frustrated.

Then in a semi-trance-like state, she began ranting, "We are the Contarini militia. The last surviving direct descendants of the first Venetian family of Venice, and our lifelong mission is to restore Venice to the golden age where merchants rule the city. Taino became a threat when he tried to protect Stephan, Mia, and his girlfriend from *our* justice code. Even though he's my uncle, he forgot to tell you I'm adopted, and he's not a Contarini."

Senn listened dumbfounded as Anna smoldered on to unbutton her scales.

"The Contis work for us. The Teatro was our little storage to move goods around. It was all working just fine until Stephan lost his marbles," Anna said with an exasperated shrug.

CHAPTER 57

THE CRUSHING LAST STRAW

"Truth is stranger than fiction, but it is because Fiction is obliged to stick to possibilities; Truth isn't."

—MARK TWAIN

Anna stopped talking mid-sentence, strode up to Senn, and stubbed her cigarette on his wrist's metal clamp, making him squirm in his chains, trying to avoid getting burnt. Amused by his recoil, Anna stood her ground and playfully traced her fingers down his muscular chest until they rested on his genitals, smirked, and said, "What a waste."

Before Senn could react, her knee rammed into his genitals with a crushing force that made him scream in pain. Anna giggled as Senn tried to lessen the pain with repeated heavy breaths from his mouth.

She was in no mood for mercy and in no hurry to kill, but Senn had to keep her engaged to get more details of her involvement.

He shouted through the numbing pain, "But Laura was innocent. Why hurt her?"

Anna lit another cigarette and wrinkled her eyebrows. "Because she saw Antonio taking care of business, which made her a risk." Anna sat, and her tone turned quite pensive, like how she used to speak to him while discussing the case.

She continued, "As you brilliantly deduced, the Teatro basement was our headquarters, and Stephan and Mia obeyed our command and ran the Teatro as an artistic cover-up."

Anna paused and sighed. "But it all changed when Stephan started fucking Laura secretly in the basement. We warned him to keep her away, but he didn't listen."

Anna sounded frustrated and agitated at the memory and chewed her nails as she spoke. Shrugging, she continued, "Anyway, Laura saw Antonio choking the bitch dead, who also made things quite complicated for me when you found her poem in the warehouse."

Senn remembered her scrawl for help in the warehouse. He butted in, "Who was she?"

"Just a petty thief who tried to sell some of our stuff without our permission," replied Anna, sounding bored. "We hate pickpockets."

"But I enjoyed dressing her up for you, " Anna said with a wicked gleam in her eyes. "You were shaking when you had to identify her body, thinking it could be Laura."

Senn stared blankly at Anna as he let the gush of hate pass through his veins.

Anna laughed, screwed her face into a jeer, and said, " Laura, Laura, Laura. She was the irritating pebble in my boots. I *ordered* Stephan to let her go, but he begged and pleaded, said he was in love and was going to marry her blah blah blah. And then he screwed it all up further by hiding her and refusing to tell us her location!"

"We were sure he'd paid Luca and Dario to smuggle her out. But they swore they had not until their last breath."

Anna stared at Senn, her eyes slowly welling with tears. "We had no choice, Senn. I swear. I can promise you it was not personal—strictly business. We could not let anyone know about our cocaine depot and transportation point. Our Albanian partners were worried and needed us to take quick, decisive action. We were desperate, Senn!"

Senn watched, horrified, as Anna's personality changed like a chameleon right before his eyes. One minute she was kneeing him in the balls, and the next, weeping like a lost teenager. She seemed highly disoriented.

Anna composed herself as her cigarette ash piled up at her feet. Her boot was slowly tapping as she gently rocked on the chair, holding her head in her hands.

She sprang up from the chair, pulled out the Glock 17 pistol, and pointed it straight at Senn's face. And, seething with anger, shouted in a sarcastic, whiny tone, "Then you, you, you, filthy son of a bitch showed up looking for your *best* friend. The fucking famous journalist on a personal rescue mission. I hate you, Senn. I hate you."

Anna pushed the pistol barrel on Senn's forehead, put both hands on the trigger, and, with eyes scorching with hate, screamed, "I HATE YOU!"

Senn froze, tightly shut his eyes, and silently chanted, '*Om Shakti*' once in his mind, ready for the bullet to blow his brains out. His body trembled with fear, and adrenaline crescendoed through his veins. He'd survived many close calls, but today, he felt the kiss of death on his lips.

Anna stood there, her whole body trembling, fingers pressed against the trigger with the barrel dug into Senn's forehead, eyes burning with a manic rage, still whispering, "I hate you. I hate you."

But after a few blood-freezing seconds, her hands eased off the trigger, and she removed the gun from his forehead, replaced it in her holster, and slumped back into the chair, exhausted and distracted.

Senn opened his eyes, his body still trembling, and saw Anna absorbed in her phone, intensely flicking through screens. She found something that made her eyes light up and break into an adoring smile. Excited, she jumped up from her chair and rushed towards Senn, tears welling again in her eyes.

In a voice cracking with emotion, she said, "I want to show you something." She turned the phone towards Senn.

What he saw made his heart sink.

It was a selfie of Anna and Antonio cuddling together on a beach.

In the background, Anna sobbed, "He was the love of my life."

As the image of him stabbing Antonio to death in the Ottagono flashed in Senn's mind, he surmised, *This is why I am here, and this is why I am still alive. I owe her the love of her life.*

CHAPTER 58

LAST RITES

If today is my last day alive, I better live.

Senn awoke to men carrying him blindfolded on a stretcher from his cell to somewhere outside.

At that instant, his body convulsed with a soul flash.

He saw himself falling from a high cliff into a hellish ocean. Senn knew it was portentous.

Despite the dire warning, Senn felt calm and grateful.

Especially since his last memory was Anna walking out and letting her men loose on him, who took turns punching and kicking him from every side until he blacked out in pain and exhaustion. He was sure they'd killed him with their blows.

Senn could smell pine trees in the crisp air and the sound of a bird in the distance. His chest ached with every breath. All he could taste in his parched mouth was dry blood as he felt the gaps where some of his teeth had broken.

But on the bright side, they'd removed his cuffs and shackles and put some clothes on him. And he could still move his fingers and toes, which was another promising sign. Was he being moved to another place?

The men walked in silence briskly as they reached an open area and placed him on the ground. The wind was much stronger here. Two men bent and lifted him by his limp arms, walked him up a step, propped him up against a pole, and tied his hands behind. The salty gust of the ocean walloped Senn's body and made him shiver.

Then a hand lifted the mask over his head. It took Senn a few seconds to focus through the fog of his swollen, bloodshot eyes but what he saw chilled him to the bone.

He was at the edge of a jagged cliff surrounded by a vast, dark ocean a few hundred feet below him. The inky sky ahead spewed lightning shards inside the angry, rain-laden clouds.

Senn turned his head and saw Anna kneeling a few feet to the right wearing a black cape, whispering something with her hands folded, and holding a silver urn. She was sobbing. Then suddenly, the sky opened, and it started pouring down.

At that instant, Senn recalled his first soul flash when he began searching for Laura. He'd seen a woman wearing a black cape on a stage in the rain. Senn thought it was Laura, but it was Anna.

He'd misread the omen about her!

As usual, his erratic soul flashes had gotten the last laugh.

Senn watched Anna grimly rise and toss the urn, watching it hurtle down the jagged edge and disappear into the ocean.

Then she raised her hand and pushed her cape off her head, revealing a shaved head and the unmistakable Venetian mafia double black wing tattoo etched right across the back of her scalp.

Anna's eyes raged as she drew a long dagger, let out a manic scream, and stabbed Senn in the stomach with all her force.

The blade tore into his body with a crunching jolt. He heard Anna laughing hysterically as she kept pushing the knife deeper into his body and shouting, "Vindicta. Vindicta. Vindicta."

Behind him, an uproar of voices chanted and repeated, "Vindicta, Vindicta. Vindicta."

Blinded by the pain and shock, Senn fell unconscious and collapsed with his head bowed and his whole body weight held up by his handcuffs on the pole.

After a few seconds, Anna raised her hands, and the crowd fell silent.

She motioned her men to untie Senn and bring his body forward to the edge of the cliff. Senn's blood, mixed with the lashing rain, flowed like a river down the cliff's edge. Anna left the dagger lodged inside him and dragged his limp body to the cliff's edge.

She leaned down, spat into his face, gave him one last menacing look, and kicked his chest to roll him off the cliff.

At that moment, Senn's eyes opened. He grabbed her foot and, with a death stare, said, "*Come die with me.*"

And before anyone could react, Senn pulled her hard, making her lurch forward, lose her balance, and fall off the edge with him.

Senn inhaled deeply as Anna's blood-curdling scream led them hurtling down the cliff together towards certain death.

Senn hit the water hard, and the impact sucked his body down. He opened his eyes and saw Anna a few feet above him, lashing underwater and trying to swim to the top.

Senn raised his hands, grabbed her leather boot, and pulled her down. She fought hard to dislodge his grip, but Senn held on until they were face to face.

He was a military-trained, no-fins free diver and knew he still had about a minute of air left in his lungs.

Anna made one last valiant attempt to unhook herself from Senn's clutches, and her scared, pleading, grey eyes looked straight into his, but suddenly, she stopped struggling, and her body went limp, and her eyes froze.

He waited for another ten seconds to be sure she was dead and then let go of her body and slowly let himself rise to the top. His head breached the surface, and he gasped his first breath of freedom.

The sky was crimson, and dawn was breaking over the horizon. Senn felt for the dagger in his stomach and realized it was gone. The force of hitting the water from the height had dislodged it.

But he didn't have much time left.

He'd lost too much blood. He pushed his body into a floating position, spread his arms, and let out a triumphant cry.

Evil had drowned, and he was free.

CHAPTER 59

THE OBITUARY OF NICHOLAS SENN

Nicholas Andreas Senn, 32, drowned on Wednesday while at sea. Born in Switzerland and raised by the world, Senn was an investigative journalist and an avid globetrotter. A graduate of Harvard Business School, Senn loved writing about and standing up against injustice in the world. He loved martial arts, photography, and spending time in nature. Please send your condolences to post box 221.

Col. Taino finished reading, put the newspaper down, and smiled at Senn lying in a hospital bed. He winked and said, "You're dead, soldier."

Senn smiled back at the colonel and mumbled a thank you from under his bandages and tubes, refueling him back to life.

The nurse walked past and drew the curtains to let the bright morning sun gush into the spacious hospital room as Taino sat across from Senn and talked gently, in a manner unlike his usual bombastic style.

"You've been in a coma for a week, Senn. I was so worried that I had to dust off that old Bible for some company. But yesterday, the doctors called me and said you're starting to move and reassured me that you'd make it." Taino's voice was soaked in relief.

He continued, "I ordered the obituary to be published as soon as we found you to get rid of the mafia flies looking for you. I hope you don't mind the language."

Senn nodded to confirm he was OK with the colonel's decision to announce his death. Given the circumstances, it was the only way.

Taino had a lot to say to bring Senn up to speed on things, so he continued talking. "It was by a bizarre stroke of luck we found you, man! We were rushing up to the castle, where Anna and her men had taken you, when a local fisherman hailed us down on the road and said they had found a body stuck in their fishing nets a few hundred feet out at sea. They thought sharks had attacked you by the bruises and cuts on your body."

Taino choked out his next words, "You were a mess."

Senn was relieved yet curious to know how Taino had discovered the truth about Anna.

As if reading his mind, Taino muttered her name under his breath like a curse and said, "I had no idea it was Anna. No bloody idea, Senn! She hid in plain sight all along! We first found unmatched DNA on the bomb in my office, along with yours, and for a moment, I thought you were involved, but then the same DNA matched with the unknown DNA we found at Luca's and Dario's apartments. That narrowed our search quickly to someone who knew you!"

Taino shook his fist and said, I had a bad feeling about Anna. Still, I refused to accept it could be her, but then on the same evening, we found CCTV footage from Dario's building and saw Anna and Antonio waiting outside on the last evening he was seen alive."

Taino slapped his knees in frustration as he related the sequence of discoveries.

He drew a hard breath. "That morning you went to her flat, I was desperate to tell you all this, but you'd escaped the safe house through the roof! I must have missed you by a few minutes. My team was racing to catch her, but she disappeared with you and her men."

Senn nodded and sighed. He, too, had missed all the signs. He knew that trust, like love, was blind.

Taino continued, "We searched her apartment and found a bedroom littered with LSD and cocaine, the same batch we found in Stephan's boat, and abundant evidence of Antonio in her apartment.

You know he was her lover, don't you?" Taino asked, frowning. "They'd been together since high school, and nobody knew."

Senn nodded and smirked. "Yes, she showed me their holiday photos just before she kicked me in the nuts."

Taino nodded grimly, dropped his voice, and, looking a little lost, said, "I knew she was adopted, but I treated her like my own daughter. I could never imagine she had such a dark secret life she hid from me, Senn."

Taino clenched his jaw and fought back tears before regaining his composure.

"Anyway, after we reached the castle, we managed to round up twenty members of her gang (including Mikkey) who'd shown up for Antonio's funeral and your sacrificial killing. They were all high on LSD when we found them. It was some weird ceremony where they all tripped on LSD as a mark of respect for Antonio, an LSD junkie."

Senn asked if he'd found Anna's body.

"Not yet, but we're still looking," he answered with a wry smile. "The tide was going out that day, so she'll probably show up on an Italian beach sometime soon."

Senn sighed, still feeling a tinge of discomfort. He was sure he'd drowned her. But he would have loved to know she was dead for sure.

There was a slight lull in the conversation, and Senn knew what was coming next.

Taino turned away from Senn and looked out the window. "We still can't find Stephan and Laura." Then Taino glanced back at Senn with a slight smile. "It's my job to ask."

Senn stared straight back at Taino and, with a slight smile, replied, "No clue, colonel." Stephan was a wanted criminal in Venice for peddling drugs for the mafia, but they both knew he had the best alibi.

Stephan and Laura were married.

Taino let out his signature booming laugh, leaned down, shook Senn's hand, and said, "OK, soldier. Let's leave it like that."

Then he walked out of the room, leaving Senn smiling back in relief and happiness.

Senn looked out of the window, and just then, a couple of bright yellow butterflies came and sat on the grill and enjoyed the sun's warmth on their shining wings. Then they flew up into the air and danced around each other before vanishing into the blue sky above.

Senn smiled, closed his eyes, and wished Laura and Stephan a lifetime of happiness.

The End.

Thank you for reading my third novel.
I hope you enjoyed it.

You can follow my projects and upcoming books on:

- https://amazon.com/author/andytravis
- https://andytravis.medium.com
- https://twitter.com/AndyTravis31
- Email: andytravis@email.com

ACKNOWLEDGMENTS

My sincere gratitude to my developmental editor Megan Records for invaluable advice on sharpening my plotlines and character motivations. A big shout out to my copy editor and proofreader, Judi Weiss, for diligently cleaning up my garbled grammar. And a bow to my designer Sarah Lahay for making the words spellbindingly vivid.

Hunted in Venice and Andy Travis remain forever grateful to all of you.

www.ingramcontent.com/pod-product-compliance
Lightning Source LLC
LaVergne TN
LVHW041147150826
845673LV00001B/89

9789083234229